There were no primeval memories in the mind of Olympus city. She was new, created within the last millennium of the continent's existence. There were no subliminal lessons in its atmosphere that the inhabitants could learn. Those lessons lay dormant in their own brains.

Shrieks in the night, howls beneath full moons, shades and shivers and the threat of mutilation and death were facts the echoes of which resounded in muted tones within the layers of the human subconscious.

Fear stalked the city, gaunt, taloned, fanged; it· wore whatever individual terror offered it. Burdensome but not nearly as destructive as the actual menace, it nevertheless scattered reason and smothered intent. The Fluger had unearthed the dread buried beneath millennia of forgetfulness. **Man must rely on instinct to survive.**

THE FLUGER

Doris Piserchia

DAW Books, Inc.
Donald A. Wollheim, Publisher

1633 Broadway, New York, N.Y. 10019

PUBLISHED BY
THE NEW AMERICAN LIBRARY
OF CANADA LIMITED

First Printing, November 1980

1 2 3 4 5 6 7 8 9

DAW TRADEMARK REGISTERED
U.S. PAT. OFF. MARCA REGISTRADA,
HECHO EN WINNIPEG, CANADA

PRINTED IN CANADA

COVER PRINTED IN U.S.A.

Chapter I

The shadow in the archway behind Addard shifted and the alien came in escorted by number four adviser. Addard was enraged. No tentacles, thank heaven, not that he had expected the assassin to have any, nor did Kam Shar own bug eyes, warty skin or anything like them, and this was why Addard was angry, or at least he supposed this was the cause of his emotion.

His outstretched hand was damp in the palm so it was just as well that the Eldoron didn't accept it but merely stood unmoving and impassive. Allergic to human sweat? Contemptuous, sneering, disgusted, afraid? The man (thing) might have been any of those, though he didn't appear to be other than patient, observant, intelligent and alert. Funny how those calm gray eyes seemed to pierce one's skull. No, the Eldoron wasn't telepathic, or so Addard had been told. Again he felt outraged and now he knew why. He worked with a bunch of fools.

Kam Shar looked exactly like a human except for his eyes, which were too intensely gray and sparkling. Then perhaps his nose was a pinch too long and thin, while his lips were too well modeled, too pink. Were the teeth sharp, blunt, broad, tiny? The man from Eldoron stood more than two meters in height, weighed about ninety kilos; a large man (creature), really, and in fact he seemed to dwarf the business office which was a part of Addard's apartment. Addard seethed, not because he was jealous or afraid but because of the fools.

"You'll report to me regularly," he said. The questions in

his mind stumbled over one another. What did aliens think of people? Did they think of them as humans? As Earthlings? What did they call Earth's dominant life form? "What am I to you?" he blurted, dismayed at himself. The fools whose task it was to advise him must be spreading their infection.

Kam Shar's voice was soft and low. His diction was perfect, his choice of words accurate. "Everyone calls his homeworld Earth or the equivalent of the word. On my planet we give either numbers or letters to the worlds with which we have contact. Yours is the equivalent of Kappa."

"Which makes me a Kappan?"

"I can call you an Earthling if you prefer."

"Or anything else you take a notion to," Addard said, immediately regretting his words and their accompanying bitterness. "No, it doesn't matter. Please think of me as a Kappan. Hopefully your business here will soon be discharged."

"Yes."

"We haven't informed our citizens of your presence. It isn't something we want to do."

Kam Shar smiled. His teeth were simply teeth, like any man's. But then he wasn't a man. "I will be discreet and remain as unobserved as possible."

"You'll catch the Fluger?"

"And kill him."

"How long will it take?"

"Not long," said Kam Shar. "I'll report to you at regular intervals." He turned and walked out.

Number four adviser, who had been sitting on a lounge, got up, crossed to the archway and looked after him.

"Who showed him how things operate?" asked Addard. "Where's he going?"

The adviser came back. "I don't know. He seems to work very independently. Since he's a galactic detective—I suppose he's actually a hit man—maybe there are no more surprises for him. How many ways are there to build cities and how many different modes of transportation and sources of information are there? I imagine he's seen them all."

"How does he strike you?"

"Impenetrable. I couldn't begin to guess what goes on in his mind."

"Alien?"

"Not especially."

He didn't like her for that, wanted her to declare the Eldoron ridiculous, intolerable and nerve-racking as he seemed to Addard.

She went away and he went back to his film viewer. Before Kam Shar's appearance he had been monitoring the condition of the city budget. At a touch of his finger on the machine's control knob, page after page of facts, figures, cautions and predictions passed before his eyes. Something would have to be done about transportation. More cabs had to be requisitioned, but first the money must come from somewhere. That had been a big chunk of glitter the vice-mayor chopped off the cube for Mr. Alien from Eldoron. A very sizeable chunk.

After he gave the intercom Randecker's name and address, it showed him in a blurry haze until the other man accepted the hail, after which the scene on the screen showed Randecker in bed.

"I worked late last night."

"Run a check on Eldoron for me," said Addard.

"What is it?"

"A planet in the Cyclone Cluster. Fourth system from the sun, third in."

"What else do you know about it?"

Addard didn't know anything else about Kam Shar's world and said so. The admission angered him. When Varone was alive he had habitually made private deals and then passed the buck on to Addard. This buck was turning up blanker than any of the others. Now Varone was dead of a heart attack and the city played host to his purchase.

The Fluger hated the city and the noise, which meant he relished what he was doing; hatred was his inspiration and his motive for living. Buried in his brain was a pebble-sized gland that released vitriol into his bloodstream as regularly as his belly demanded sustenance, a condition or a happenstance that came about when his species was developing on the homeworld. Hateful place, Fluga. Hateful people. The Fluger loved it. In order to survive, he and his kind needed to be competitive, untrusting and untrustworthy.

7

Corradado was big—four hundred kilos, five meters long, four thick legs, lithe yellow body, blunt head, numerous teeth, eyes tawny and full of guile. He was adventuresome and curious and had stowed away on a drone, one of the mechanically driven ships that visited his world to delve for ore and precious stones. It had brought him to this place, which was inhabited by unintelligent life forms that shrieked and tried to run away from him. With zest he had been showing them what his species was like. The primary nature of his id was to seek out and challenge with all the cunning and fury of which he was capable. He was omnivorous.

Now he prowled in a cab tunnel and snarled at the lights, the glittering tile, the shiny tracks, the distant sounds and the recollection of scurrying life forms. The latter were objects of which he approved, particularly when they gave little bellows of terror before using their puny legs to try to escape from him.

Whistles in the distance made him growl low in his massive throat, made him feel inclined to ascend a tiled wall and creep along the ceiling. He found that creeping was boring since there was nothing to the activity besides crossing one clean tile brick after another. Flexing his claws and then retracting them so that all his suckers were distended, he began racing upside down along the ceiling of the tunnel at top speed in a straight line toward a little machine that tooted and zipped along unconcerned. It carried a passenger.

The front of the cab was transparent, so the man had a clear view of the tunnel ahead. At first it appeared to him that a section of the ceiling had broken and was hanging down, and he grabbed a communicator from the wall and yelled something into it. Then he grasped the brake cord and yanked hard. It wouldn't have mattered if the cab had smashed full force into Corradado, who was built like a tank and didn't know what caution was. He would simply have plowed through the front pane and ripped the passenger to pieces, which is what he did no sooner than the machine had skidded to a halt. After he finished mauling the corpse he demolished the vehicle, the tracks beneath it and a section of the side wall. Then he loped away to find a place where he could enjoy a moment or two of solitude.

On his journey he met with an obstacle, a wall and a sealed archway, which he splintered. The farther he went in that direction the more walls and closed archways he encountered. Ruining them all, angered because he was naturally antagonistic at all times, he approached a last and final partition more powerfully constructed than the rest, thick and resistant, tough where there was no obvious reason for it, stubborn and unyielding enough to further enrage him. He used his best series of claw swipes and head butts to ram his way through.

It was his turn to shriek as he crashed out of the north side of the city into empty air. Bellowing with rage, he contorted his body and made wild grappling motions with his legs. His flailing left rear appendage touched something, and with lightning speed he dug in with a single claw of his foot. The nail was yanked to its entire length but it held, so that his long body stopped plummeting and began swinging back and forth. His foot was paining him so he stilled himself, made his body dangle inertly while at the same time he assessed the situation. It seemed he was clinging to a flagpole. Luckily for him it was unreasonably thick with a diameter of at least two meters and it jutted way out from the building, if that was what the structure could be called.

The Fluger would never admit that he was capable of flawed logic or idiocy, hence he stopped thinking about the fact that he had known the shape of the city, had been aware that somewhere in the cab tunnel he was bound to run into an exterior partition. Olympus was built a kilometer high in some places. From a distance it looked like a series of 0's stuck up in the sky upon two pillars, somewhat like a surrealistic rainbow. There were ten 0's in all, well-balanced with modern and clean apartments within their walls, besides all the other things of which a city normally boasted, even speedy transportation at all times for the squealing little inhabitants. Aside from his other criticisms of the place, Corradado thought the same color of pale green everywhere had been an uninspired choice on someone's part. He preferred deep, rich colors such as purple, vermilion and black.

Dangling, thinking rapidly, he easily raised up to grasp the pole with both paws. After working his way to the apartment veranda, he kicked the pole into the clouds below. His gorge

9

rose as vertigo overcame him. For a few minutes he staggered about the veranda as he sought to wipe his mind clean of thoughts of great height, falling, smashing against hard ground. He didn't know whether or not the fall would kill him, but it was another side of Olympus and its people that he hated. They weren't afraid of high places.

The man inside the apartment was fast on his feet, courageous and not given to standing about pondering imminent disaster. When the big Fluger poked its head into his business office he turned and ran through the nearest archway, not to the cab depot below his bedroom but straight into the next apartment. At that, he wasn't so courageous, having momentarily diverted the predator by presenting another prey in the form of an astonished woman in the act of bathing, but perhaps he suffered from mind stall and didn't know what he was doing.

He ought to have tried the cab depot and the lower tunnels, which were filled with cubbyholes, maintenance rooms and dark shafts. Both he and the wet woman broke the same glass pane as they flew through it, propelled by the same rapier-like claw attached to Corradado and, since Olympus was so modern that nearly everything in the city was soundproof, their cries went unheard as they pitched headlong and due south for approximately one kilometer.

A slum boy named Hulian roasted a ten-kilo rat over hot coals and contemplated the fortune which was bound to come to him sometime in the near future. His ship would come in, the pot at the end of the rainbow would be his, the sunken treasure would float ashore at his feet. Why was he so optimistic? Because he was thirteen and in good health due to the fat rats, fruit and vegetables which were his daily fare.

Hulian was black but that wasn't why he was poor. Addard was also black, as were many citizens of Olympus; their citizenship was the reason why they were well-to-do if not downright wealthy. One day Hulian would receive his right to live in the sky-metropolis. He would move into one of the luxurious apartments, find work suitable to his varied talents and then there would be no more rats, no more filth or filthy companions, no street language and dreariness.

10

Now he cooked his dinner beside one of the pillars holding up the city and minded his own business. Half a kilometer to his right was an entrance into Olympus, a small complex staffed by employees who dealt with slum visitors during daylight hours, gave them briefings on the procedures for citizenship application, dispensed brochures that depicted life in the big town. Most visitors were only interested in how soon they could be admitted into one of the high 0's, having already read dozens of brochures and viewed hundreds of photographs of the parks, apartments, utility complexes, industrial units, bureaucratic blocks, cathedrals, synagogues, temples, schools, etc. Most had come from other cities, or rather their slums. When one wasn't born into civilization it was a long and tedious process to get there by annexation. Life in a city greatly depended upon checks and balances, which meant that a thousand extra bodies could conceivably throw the status quo out of kilter, not to mention the fact that bureaucrats were afflicted with leaden feet.

Hulian was willing to go by the book as long as he believed such a course would prove beneficial to him, but when he decided otherwise he would do something else. Olympus was his city because he had been born in her shadow. He didn't want to live in any other, though he had traveled across country and seen Superior, Yosemite, Carlsbad, even Everglade way down in the swamp. After he became an Olympian he could ride in speedy underground cabs and visit Troy, Rome, Saxony and Orio. It was incredible to think that a trip abroad in one of those special cabs required no more than twenty or twenty-five minutes.

He cooked his dinner, dreamed of future glory and was unaware of the havoc being played inside the entry complex to the city he loved. Knowing nothing of Flugers, Eldorons or interstellar travel, he nodded and dreamed, allowed his head to lean against the beloved steel so close to him and for a little while he slept. As he did so the Fluger pierced the visitor's complex, dispensed with the personnel, burst into the open and raced straight toward him.

He was scarcely awake when the big alien passed him, would never know why the swipe of the claw only took out his left eye as he turned to see what raced across the dusty ground with such speed. It could have been his head that rolled in the dirt, or Corradado might have come to a full stop and gutted him like a deer vanquished by a wolf. Probably the Fluger was sated with flesh and blood, or likely he was tired of being cooped up and wanted to taste some open country. The Earth boy wasn't significant but of course no aborigine could go untouched by the great Corradado, and so the Fluger relieved Hulian of one little eye and continued racing across the ground of what had once been called the United States, state of New York, city of Manhattan.

Using the sleeve of his shirt for a bandage around his head, Hulian staggered home to get help. When he arrived there he found the place a shambles and guessed that whatever the thing was that had wounded him had also done this. The old man who had shared his shack was dead, ripped from chin to groin and tossed through the tin ceiling like fodder. Everyone in the shantytown was dead. Corradado had missed no one, had left not a single abode standing. In the time it had taken Hulian to stumble there from the stoop of Olympus the big creature made a graveyard of his home.

All night he lay beside the old man's stiffening corpse and sopped his leaking eye socket. His only fear was that he would bleed to death or perish from infection. One thing he had to accomplish before going down into the final hole was to slit the throat of the monster that had hurt him and killed the only person he loved.

There were no primeval memories in the imaginary mind of Olympus. She was new, created within the last millennium of the continent's existence. There were no subliminal lessons in its atmosphere that the inhabitants could learn. Those lessons lay dormant in their own brains. Shrieks in the night, howls beneath full moons, shades and shivers and the threat of mutilation and death were facts the echoes of which resounded in muted tones within the layers of the human subconscious. Forgotten since man decided to be merciful to his own kind, they would be brought to the surface of every thinking mind.

Fear stalked the city, gaunt, taloned, fanged; it wore whatever individual terror offered it. The fact was the fear wasn't alive. It merely seemed so. Burdensome but not nearly as destructive as the actual menace, it nevertheless scattered reason and smothered intent. The Fluger had unearthed the dread buried beneath millennia of forgetfulness. Man must rely on instinct to survive.

Chapter II

Addard sat in Council and couldn't believe his ears. With all the fancy equipment they had, they still must play games. "You let that ship dump an uninspected cargo?" he said for the third time, wincing when Monkwell grinned again. Monkwell was an easy-going man, who assumed that everyone was his friend, even his superior, who happened to be in a bad mood. He didn't know Addard disliked his red hair and freckles.

"Not in a century or a millennium. But that Fluger came off the ship just the same."

"It was your department's job," said Addard.

"So are a million other things. The cargo was inspected."

"By whom?"

"A foreman."

"Name?" said Addard.

"Roxey."

"Now we're getting somewhere, because for a change I'm one up on you. I personally checked on the landing foremen and I remember Roxey. He's as blind as a mole, sees by a radar unit."

"Which reads a cargo item as well as or better than two eyes," said Monkwell.

"True, if you're only interested in the size and weight of

13

an item, but supposing one of them is on the move, like, say, a monster of an alien with four legs?"

Monkwell shrugged. "It was logged in three different places. Roxey did his job. We just didn't catch it."

The white-haired man named Ennesto spoke up. "That's past history."

"It is, and so is the next point I'm about to bring up, but you understand I like to know these things," said Addard. It wouldn't do any good to be angry but then he couldn't help himself. He had been trying to unseat Monkwell for over a year but so far he hadn't succeeded. He suspected that his third adviser was a certifiable moron who had paid somebody to cover up the records. "I want to know who brought the Eldoron in," he said. "I mean everyone involved."

Garly laughed and Addard wanted to lean across the table and hit him. Trust the little cynical wizard to mock the most serious thing that had happened in Olympus since the tidal wave of 2020. Not that the first adviser hadn't good cause for derision, since the logical alternative was rage or panic or both. They were the major legislative body, somewhat like a president and his cabinet of olden times, and they were expected to haul the collective chestnuts out of the fire. Yesterday.

"Don't slight me for saying so," said Garly, "but I know for a fact that Varone told one of his messenger boys to get him a good assassin from another planet, so the messenger boy got on the outercom and called the first agent he could find on the list."

"That's it?" said Addard.

"Right."

"We have no bio on Kam Shar, no psychological profile, no emotional sketch, no anatomical blueprint?"

"We don't even know what he likes to eat," said Monkwell. His grin was back.

"I want all that," said Addard. "You get it for me, the three of you. That's why you're paid, because you assist me. That's why you were selected. Do it. Not only do I want a mountain of data on Kam Shar but I want to know everything about that Fluger."

"Nobody dumped that on us except fate," said Ennesto.

14

"The drone ship was outfitted with scanners but he still got aboard."

"No matter how he got here he was dumped on all of us. You'd better understand that, and not only on the four of us but on every Olympian who wants to defend himself."

"Maybe we can quit worrying," said the old man. "Possibly we can unload our problem on Superior. He was headed toward them last night."

"That was last night," said Garly.

Addard ran the tips of his fingers through his short hair. "He's coming back our way. Defense chased him with some tanks and made him mad."

"Couldn't they put a dent in him?" asked Monkwell. His expression matched that of the others now, was subdued and even worried. Perhaps he was thinking of his new wife.

"He sticks close to slum towns so they can't bomb him. I think he has the message. If he stays in the open we're bound to get him."

"And he can get back here a lot faster than he can get to Superior," said Garly.

After they had all gone, Addard called Randecker.

"I'm getting all kinds of stalls."

"What do you mean?" said Addard.

"Either nobody out there knows what an Eldoron is or they just don't want to open up."

"I've got to know what I'm dealing with here. Any day now this city is going to wake up and realize what it's facing. What can you do for me?"

"There's supposed to be a research outfit on Lambda doing a sort of stellar genealogy. I guess if anyone knows what we want, they do. I've been trying to contact them."

"Keep trying. Let me know as soon as you learn anything."

Randecker cleared his throat. "If you ask me it's an every-man-for-himself situation. Why don't you quit?"

"Will that keep the Fluger from coming into my apartment? Or yours?"

Corradado lay on the rooftop of an intact shanty and allowed the sun's rays to warm his sinewy carcass. He felt relaxed and rested. In a few more minutes he would head back toward

Olympus where he intended to create mayhem. Flattening slum towns was satisfying enough for him, but there was more excitement when he did his thing in closer quarters where the adversary became paralyzed at sight of him.

The sun made him almost drift off so that for brief moments he seemed to be back home in the rock maze. He was surrounded by his dead siblings whom he had slain. His father stood on a stone pedestal and told him to go, that even a Fluger must learn to control the flow of his rage, that the bones of the corpses would be strewn in front of the maze entrance as a reminder to the last born of this family that he was forever banished.

Corradado's yellow eyes flicked open, glistened with fresh intensity because of the dream. By now the aborigines of Olympus had girded their loins for war and were gathering their laughable weapons for an advance into the outlands. It was well. All was well. Vitriol, acid and corrosion coursed aplenty through his circulatory system, firing his already alert brain, signaling to his muscular mass until he arose and leaped from the roof in a single graceful motion. The sun bounced off his sleek hide as warmly as it had ricocheted from the bent tin roof.

The Earth boy named Hulian took to the alleys with a familiarity born of practice and necessity. His sword hung from a rope tied around his waist, dragged on the ground, clattered against stones, impeded his progress but for no price would he have left it behind. With its finely honed blade he would sever the jugular of the yellow monstrosity he pursued.

Untutored, illiterate, keen of intellect, Hulian knew of the lights in the sky but it never entered his head that the beast ahead of him was not really a beast but an intelligent organism from another planet.

Dusk was a fast plunging wave that engulfed his small figure and washed away his scent with a slight breeze. He lingered on the outskirts of a rock mountain, loathe to leave its protection until he knew where the yellow monster was. All day he had trailed it through towns, woods and quarries and by now he knew that it was aware of his presence. Occasionally it stopped to let him catch up, so he rightly guessed it had already chosen the spot where it intended to blot the world clean of him, except that he had different plans and would make certain he wasn't in the appointed place when Corradado made his move.

The time would come when the boy knew the Fluger almost intimately, just as he would be familiar with another stranger named Kam Shar, but for now he knew nothing of any Eldoron and supposed that Corradado was some kind of freak tiger-bear.

A smell came with the night wind, a redolent scent unlike that of any animal he had ever tracked, and in his day of slum towns and hunger he had tracked plenty across the wilderness of eastern United States. There were the rats, cats, wolves, bears, boars, bison, each suitable to eat when the belly was empty, but the thing ahead of him in the rocks, the large specimen with neither father nor mother in any of the land about, that one was tutu. It was unknown and it smelled like nothing born to wilderness or captivity. Tutu needed a bath. The Earth boy would see that he got one in his own blood.

Bedding down in a cavity between smooth stones, he waited for sunlight, aware that the creature prowled in the shadows not far away. If Tutu wanted to battle it out in the morning the human would be ready.

What Hulian didn't realize was that Corradado knew exactly where he was and could have blasted the rocks to powder with his powerful paws. However, he was more interested in the small army advancing toward the quarry.

In the morning a chagrined Captain Echea guided his tanks into the open, muttering all the while because the defense chief had insisted that he take charge of an activity which was beneath him. He wouldn't mind a fracas with a force from Superior or Everglade but this animal was some kind of mutant that had escaped from a zoo. Or from somewhere. Whatever, it wasn't worthy of Olympus' finest war machines. The tanks were so versatile they could almost fly yet none of their weight or firepower had been sacrificed on the drawing board.

Number three vehicle scattered boulders like pebbles, tossed them out of the way, and quickly too, so that it went boring into the quarry like an impatient mole, only to retreat when it met with a frosty yellow eye followed by an unbelievable

17

left hook. The driver never once suspected this might be the Unindentified Killing Object that had been loose in Olympus for the past few weeks. Only those with firsthand knowledge knew what the UKO looked like, and for some reason they weren't broadcasting it.

Now Echea knew the battle was for real and that it wasn't a game. He was happy to get a little of even this kind of action but it seemed to him a ludicrous ploy to throw ten modern tanks against an animal. Rather, he would have taken an archery team after the thing. The ten steel machines he had brought with him would make mincemeat of it in nothing flat.

To the fore and never mind how asinine the maneuver seemed. It wouldn't take long and then Echea could do what he had made up his mind to do that morning: find his wife, wherever she was and see if she was willing to produce the child they had pledged when they were sworn in as a married couple. How long had it been since she left the apartment adjoining his and went to visit friends? He thought it might have been two or three years.

They could have gotten the tanks there by airlift from the parking site, but the defense chief ordered them down the els and out into the dust on their own power, which wasn't inconsiderable since they could cruise at a hundred kilometers an hour without losing any of their defensive effectiveness. Echea kept his eye on the *tev*, shifting once in a while to the computer readouts showing where the animal was at any given moment. Nothing living in the area was as big or as fast and agile, so it wasn't difficult picking him out of the readouts of all the other life forms being monitored.

The Captain kept thinking of his wife, Laray, as he dropped his vehicle back and signaled for number two to go forward and lay one on the enemy's head or rear end, depending upon which way he jumped. It was unusual, his thinking about Laray, for he hadn't done that but infrequently lately. In fact, he hadn't really thought of her since he decided to investigate her fascination with astral projection and became an astro himself.

Echea could have done it right then, gone out of his body in that instant and left the tank and its crew to muddle about in the filthy dirt and undergrowth of the outside while his hulk slumped without feeling a thing. Of course he shouldn't do it, so he didn't, but he chased the yellow animal and hated every minute of it because he had thought about projecting and now wanted to do it so badly his hands trembled on the control panel. He tasted sweat on his upper lip. Maybe his superior was right and he should take a couple of weeks off and go abroad for a rest. After all, if he and Laray were going to get together again she had to be brought down to earth, so to speak, and he couldn't help her as long as he himself was on the wing.

The enemy wasn't behaving according to plan or prediction (that huge enemy, and how had he grown so large?). It made like a giant flea and hopped all over the place ahead of the eggs. While they were harmlessly exploding, he was ten meters distant and had actually begun attacking vehicles.

Among all the things Echea didn't know was the fact that Fluga was such a heavy planet that whatever it bore was immensely dense. He wouldn't have believed it even if it had been explained to him that Fluga's great gravity made her offspring comfortably light and powerful on a planet such as Earth.

The Captain kept abreast of the information pouring from the computer but he was mainly interested in the *tev*, not that what he saw on the screen initiated any new plans for maneuvering on his part. He was simply astonished and dismayed at what the animal was doing. It ripped the entire right track from number three vehicle, and not with a great deal of effort either, but casually loped in from the side and gave the strip a swipe with one claw. The track came off in pieces that flew in all directions while the beast ran around to the front and bit the main gun and its turret off the machine. The tank bucked like a horse, probably rattling the crew so that they couldn't throw flames or gas at the Fluger, who leaped onto the top and tore away the lid with its teeth. Echea's vehicle moved erratically as he watched the animal dive through the hole and disappear down inside number three tank.

He hadn't long to wonder what would happen next because only two or three minutes passed and Corradado came through the side of number three as if it were made of cardboard. While Echea fought mind stall and tried to cancel out imaginative scenes of gore and horror, the enemy raced through and over thorn bushes and rocks to attack number one tank.

The crew threw everything they had but it was all evaded by the yellow demon, flames, eggs, gas, missiles, not a single item hitting him or even coming near him. What they needed, what they believed they needed, was a cauldron all around the tank, but they hadn't enough of anything and they could do nothing to prevent the Fluger from eventually coming in after them.

At first they tried to fight back while he bit and ripped the outside to shreds and shards, but they were nearly lethargic by the time he came down the hole like an evil-eyed snake. He was in no hurry. There was Robey at the main gun. The animal took his belly in his mouth and bit him in half while Robey's hands beat on his snout like a drummer. Blood hit the floor as if dumped from a bucket. The technician named Wacker slipped in it, fell on his stomach and stayed that way as Corradado placed a forepaw on his head and pressed until it flattened out. Echea was screaming about astros and the baby he and Laray had promised faithfully they would bear, and he thought the alien grinned as it reared up ever so slightly and took him in a light hug while its teeth sank into his face and tore it away from his skull.

The only way the demoralized tank force could hit the enemy was with a lucky guess, and he worked at it to make certain they didn't produce one. Their guidance systems worked perfectly, but when their eggs landed he wasn't where he should have been. Faster than a jack rabbit he darted in and out of the quarry, attacked a tank and dispatched it or at least put it out of commission with two or three blows, leaped high in the air to get out of the way of horizontal fire. He wasn't human or natural and, though the tank operators sensed as much, they couldn't reverse their lifelong conditioning sufficiently to attack with any effectiveness. They kept firing at and advancing upon him as if he were an overgrown creature of earthly capacities. Had they but known, they couldn't have harmed a hair of him with any of their weapons.

His favorite ploy was to get on top of a tank and rip it apart while the other operators debated about firing upon a fellow machine. By the time it occurred to them that no one in the vehicle was still alive, the yellow wrecker was gone and speeding across the ground at a blinding pace, leaping to the top of another tank, popping the lid or wrenching loose the armor and hurling it away. Obviously, Corradado had fought wars before, and just as obviously, he knew the difference between men and metal, seeming to prefer the former and the sounds they made as they died.

Having already changed his mind about meeting the tank force before it left the vicinity of Olympus, the Fluger again altered his plans and headed toward the city. Four crippled machines followed him.

Once he circled around a high hill and attacked from the rear, demolishing the last one at his leisure, pulling the crew apart like lint. Climbing inside the driver's compartment, he tried to manipulate the controls but they were so smashed he couldn't make sense of the dials.

Something had happened to Hulian during the battle, which prevented him from fully appreciating the extent of Corradado's victory, something to do with his eye, or rather the socket where an eye had been. The hole burned like a hot coal and a foul smell came from the rag covering it. His flesh was beginning to rot. The wound wasn't healing.

Fired with a final energy, he made his good eye do the work of two, kept the tanks in sight and at the same time managed to make out the rocks and crevices in the quarry well enough to gain headway. Vaguely he realized that the tutu had circled around to bite off part of a tread on one of the tanks. He knew he was practically out on his feet and needed to sleep but he couldn't stop now, mustn't stay here while the tanks and the tutu sailed off to the city in the clouds.

He lost his sword somewhere along the way, or possibly he loosened it in his delirium, for it dragged and impeded his progress. Like a drunk or a desert rat sighting water, he stumbled, croaking and groaning, across bramble bushes and climbed onto the rear gun of the last tank. Straddling its broad roundness, he hugged the protrusions on the turret. The tutu was too strong for him and the knowledge made him weep. At least for now the war had to be called. Swordless, so weak he could scarcely hang onto his seat, he feebly cursed the day of his birth.

21

He made a great deal of noise because of his pain, but it alerted no one since there wasn't anybody in the vicinity who could hear him. The tank crews were isolated by soundproofing, and Corradado considered him no more significant than one of the fleas seeking asylum in his short fur.

Olympus was massive, shaped like a rainbow with ten 0's strung across its top. Thirty million people lived within its wholesome confines, brought there by the necessity or whims of their forebears, who had populated the northeastern section of the continent.

The automatic control systems in the three tanks carried them to a portion of a gigantic wall that seemed to stretch everywhere. A door opened mechanically to allow them to enter. They did so unmolested, their enemy having gone to another section where the wall wasn't so thick, and there he made his own doorway. He had lost interest in the machines and their paranoid crews.

By the time the tanks reached their destination in the parking lot, Hulian was unconscious, flaccidly sagging against cold metal and, in a manner of speaking, dead to the world. The crews climbed from their places into tubular els that took them to upper levels.

Meanwhile, the vehicles shed their armament into gleaming troughs. One by one the eggs rolled away. Stretched across one shiny specimen was the black boy whose position on the gun had been disturbed by the jostlings as the tank unloaded. He neither knew nor cared that he was being transported into the darker sections of Olympus, in fact down into its bowels underground, nor did he see the light diminish as his speed increased. Occasionally his feet hit the edge of the trough and once he nearly rolled between his egg and the one following, but the mechanics of Arms Security operated smoothly so that his body more or less maintained a level balance.

By the time the bombs were stashed in their niches with the thousands of other bombs in the storage shed, he was stirring toward consciousness. He was in number three stack, number eighteen slot with some fifty stacks above him.

He came partially awake. Immediately he was relieved that full consciousness eluded him. Pain came in searing waves that exploded through his brain and made him groan. Perhaps

22

he screamed. He lay on his face on something hard and metallic, while all around him stretched a graveyard full of unyielding objects. His searching hand failed to find an answer to his unspoken question. He had forgotten about the tanks, bombs, tutu and even the city. For an instant, while he stared blindly into blackness, he smelled the smell of dying flesh, remembering it was his own. He gave what he believed would be his last living sound before lapsing into a light coma.

He thought he was dreaming when someone turned him over. Someone had climbed down the stacks and crawled across all those bombs to see what it was in there that was making so much noise. With his good eye he glared up into a pair of sparkling gray diamonds. No, that couldn't be right. They were just eyes. But that couldn't have been right either since no one had eyes like that, besides which the man had a pair of wings similar to a bat or a bird, large appendages curling around his long body and touching the boy's cheeks like downy feathers.

Those eyes, like gems that never stopped glittering, around and in and out, never dimming, worked so hard while the feathers felt so soft, and the breast beneath his cheek was solid and warm. That sensation almost brought him out of it, nearly shocked him awake but he was too sick so he remained in a kind of twilight while the man picked him up, crawled out of the stack, hugged him close and flew up and upward into the blackness. It was done effortlessly, and all of a sudden the world was inhabited by one more tutu. This was the second unknown in Hulian's experience, a man with sparkling eyes who had wings and could fly.

The remainder of the dream wasn't frightening. The boy flew through darkness, went through a number of doors, was carried along several lightless corridors, stopped in an antiseptic place where he sat in a chair while the tutu with the wings and diamonds examined his putrefying eye socket. It was a silly dream, too many changes occurring too abruptly; the tutu didn't have wings anymore but looked like everyone else now. Or almost.

He dreamed that his eye socket was cleaned and scraped before the new eye was placed in the cavity. He saw where the new one had been stored in a small receptacle in a cabinet

23

full of eyes, eyelids, little pieces of eyes, minuscule tubes and loops of flesh with diagrams on the front of the receptacles showing how they went behind the facial cavities and inside the brain.

His dream showed him tiny instruments that connected his new orb to the tubes and loops within his head, and he stopped groaning and laughed to think of how the big yellow tutu had been outdone by the other tutu with the gentle hands and the interested manner. During the procedure the boy reached out and touched one of the white hands. The tutu stopped what he was doing and stared down at him with a quiet expression.

"Don't pity me," said Hulian. "We can't be friends if you do that."

Afterward he didn't dream anymore, sank into what might have been a coma or deep sleep, but it didn't matter at all to him since he was probably still out there by the quarry, straddling a tank gun and bawling that he was dying of acute infection. The winged man was part of his delirium and so was the new eye. All he had to do was raise his hand and feel the encrusted rag, all that remained of necessity was for him to take a sniff and he would smell his own rot. He tried but his hands wouldn't work and his nose was clogged with the odor of medicine.

Chapter III

Roxey picked up the kid a quarter kilometer away, stumbling, falling, staggering as he blundered through the turnstiles leading to northbound cabs. He waited and finally the kid got close enough for him to grab and haul erect.

"I know everything about you, from the fact that you aren't a citizen to the texture of the duds on your back," he said. "And their odor. And your odor. Phew! Everything but their color."

"Don't tell me you're color-blind too," said Hulian. The words were little more than a weak croak.

"What does that mean?"

"It ought to be obvious. How about telling me where the hospital is?" The boy tried pulling away but the man hung onto him.

"Which one?"

"There's more than one?"

"More than a thousand."

"I have to find one in particular."

"What you have to do is get thrown back outside where you belong."

"Why do you look at me so funny?"

"I'm not looking at you at all," said Roxey. "I'm blind as a bat."

Hulian jerked free and ran into a small room filled with visiphones of every shape and size. Most of them were blank, but one kept up a continual racket as the image on the screen talked and finally began to yell. "Roxey! Roxey! This is Garly. If you don't answer in five seconds you're fired!"

"Now I'm wondering if you're also stupid besides being a wetback," Roxey said. Instead of coming into the room, he paused in the archway. "I know exactly where you are. If you move your right hand another centimeter you'll scorch it on an open lead on that set."

Looking at the exposed wire, Hulian said, "How do you know that? You said you were blind."

"Being a wetback and a little criminal, you don't know about modern inventions. Come on out and I'll show you my radar unit."

It was a small, rectangular box and fit in his shirt pocket, a marvel of wires and creativity sending out sound waves that made contact with every object heavier than air and relayed signals to the miniature receivers in Roxey's ears.

"Don't think I learned to use this thing overnight," he said. He was a large, heavy man with black hair, ugly features and a way of making people think he was unintelligent. "I remember after the first time I used it I fractured my fist against a wall because I thought I'd never get the hang of it."

Hulian weaved on his feet. "What do I care how long it took you to learn it?"

"Hey, are you all right?"

"What do you care? What's it to you?"

"Wise, aren't you? Well, just imagine ten or twenty people simultaneously giving you a word to define, sometimes thirty or forty people or even a hundred. That's how the signals come into my ears from every direction. I'm getting dozens from you, for instance. You're about one-sixty-five centimeters in height, you weigh about fifty-four kilograms, your hair is short and curly, features small and regular, your pants are filthy and they're ripped, your shirt has no sleeves or collar and it's grimy, your feet are bare—"

"And you're color-blind."

Roxey chuckled. "That's about the only thing I can't see."

"You and the tutu."

"The unknown. Don't think I never heard that word before. I know plenty."

"You bet."

Roxey touched a button on the intercom so that he became visible to Garly. "Yes, sir?"

"Where have you been? Never mind. I want you to take a crew and get down to west subquarter. The Fluger's back in again and I want the damage repaired."

"Mr. Varone gave me specific orders—"

"He's dead. Heart attack."

"Oh," said Roxey. It meant Garly was number-one adviser to the mayor now and it also meant Garly was his boss. For that matter, everyone in politics was his boss. "I'll get down there right away," he said. "What'll I do with this wetback?"

"Drop him with an agency. Maybe Monkwell's people are in their offices for a change. Give him to one of them."

Roxey took Hulian home with him. They both went through a turnstile, down a short flight of stairs and stepped into a waiting cab. It was just spacious enough for the two of them, clean and comfortable, capable of attaining a speed of three hundred kilometers an hour, running along its private track in

26

a gradual ascent that took it to the westernmost 0 at the top of Olympus. They were in Section One, Level One. They were on the mount.

Hulian already knew that if he entered the left side of the archway indicated by Roxey the lights inside the apartment wouldn't go on, so he stayed behind the big man and went in on the right. The walls became white and still whiter, illuminating every corner of the modernly equipped office.

"Come on in," the blind man said, and Hulian followed him into the living room, which was also white and glitteringly antiseptic. There was a white sofa that sat against the wall and went all the way around the room, several stuffed footstools were scattered about, metal bookshelves covered two walls above the couch; by the pressing of a button the shelves moved horizontally and vertically, bringing any book down to hand level. In one corner was a pool table.

Roxey left the room, returned with a small box, had Hulian sit down and placed a square pad on the inside of his right wrist.

"Don't get excited. You won't feel a thing. This will check your vital functions, take your temperature and give your blood a quick read."

"What for?" said Hulian.

"To see if you're sick."

"I'm not sick, but I was. I'm recuperating."

Roxey agreed with him a few minutes later when the health checker had done its job. "You had some kind of infection, didn't you?"

Sighing, Hulian nodded. His eyelids drooped. He was tired, the couch was soft and he didn't know what to make of this big man who seemed reluctant to see the last of him.

"You can watch the *tev*. I'll bet you've never seen anything like it. In fact I know you haven't. Why don't you do yourself a favor and stay put? If someone with any authority out there spots you, they'll toss your pork back to the slums."

"What if I don't care one way or the other?"

"Me either, kid. If you're not here when I get back tonight it'll be all the same to me. I would've dumped you already only I'm in a hurry to get to work."

27

"It doesn't make sense," Randecker said to Addard. He spoke on a scrambled line via intercom. "Just because that Fluger is from another planet doesn't mean everything about it has to be alien."

"Well, is it?" asked Addard.

"Just about. His destructiveness is a compulsion that accelerates in intensity."

"What does that mean?"

"He isn't satisfied with simply tearing something up. It means he won't eventually go on about his business. He has the personality of an atom bomb. He wants the whole show."

"Are you telling me he'll try to destroy all of Olympus?"

"His kind wouldn't have a planet if it weren't made out of incredibly tough elements that resist corrosion and wholesale mayhem. In a nutshell, this big pup likes it here because it's so flimsy. He's a tiger in a paper bag and we're kidding ourselves if we hope he won't break out and in and out and in until the place looks like a sieve."

"So that's why Varone did it," said Addard.

"What?"

"He already collected this information, obviously. It's why he contacted a space agency to hire an assassin. Instead of checking with me first to see if I had another opinion, he just went ahead and did it. That was typical of him. So all right, now we know something about our number one alien. What about number two?"

Randecker shrugged. "I'm working on him but even with my own equipment and the privacy you gave me it isn't easy. There's nobody in my hair and that's nice but it doesn't seem to help. Either that research institute on Lambda is shy about telling secrets or it feels sorry for us because we hired ourselves an Eldoron."

Checking through the apartment, Hulian found a bathroom and bedroom. They were small; living space in Olympus had been sacrificed so that everything else could be large. Once a citizen left his quarters he no longer had cause to feel confined because the walkways at the top of the 0's had three lanes in both directions and, when the weather was good, the skylights were opened for sun and fresh air.

There was nothing to eat in the apartment so he studied the maps in Roxey's office. Only one showed the layout of the entire city, but he couldn't read the words on the little arrows. Another map showed the immediate area, was much larger and illustrated. He knew what eating areas looked like, having already seen a few on his trek from the park where the tutu with the gray eyes had left him unconscious on a bench and on the road to good health.

Thinking of the tutu made him raise his hand and outline his left eye socket with a careful finger. He still found it difficult to believe there wasn't a bloody, hollow cave there, found it uncanny to stare about at things through an eye that had belonged to someone who was probably dead. It might as well have been his own eye, so perfectly did it function. There was only one thing wrong with it. It was blue.

Rested and confident that he could find the nearest kitchen, he left the bedroom and tried to find the front door, but where it had once been there was now a blank wall. Remembering how Roxey had told him to walk in a straight line in the middle of the living room if he wanted out, he did so and immediately a panel slid away in front of him and there was the open archway leading to the outside walks.

Relatively speaking it was bedlam out there. Inside Roxey's home everything was soundproofed, but outside where hundreds of people walked, strolled or ran it was a different situation. One of the walks appeared to be exclusively for joggers in sports clothes so Hulian stayed on number three path, or the inside strip next to opposing traffic. No one paid much attention to him for everyone was dressed differently, some impeccably in shiny suits, some carelessly, while most were casual in trousers, shirts, and canvas shoes.

The kitchen was an automatic food dispensary on a large boulevard. The walls were decorated with drawers that gave out cereals, soups, sandwiches, hot plates, salads, fruit, drinks and desserts, all at the touch of a button. Unable to read the labels on the compartments, Hulian used some of the coins he had taken from the top of Roxey's bureau, pressed a button at random and watched as the lid opened and a fish plate slowly rose from somewhere in a column below the street.

"Why are you dressed so shabbily?" said the man next to him. "Are you an actor?"

Stuffing food into his mouth and keeping his head down so that his eyes couldn't be seen, Hulian nodded.

"You shouldn't be in this area in your costume. It sets a bad example for other children."

This surprised Hulian and made him realize he had yet to see one Olympian child. "Yes, you're right," he said, remembering the lessons of an old man who lay underground in a ruined slumtown. "It's just that I'm with a group."

The man took an apple from a dispenser and went away, leaving the boy to mull over future strategies. As long as he had coins he could have food at the kitchens, which didn't seem to care whether or not he was a citizen; he had free lodging at Roxey's place if he wanted it and he was beginning to get his strength back.

There was now a crowd inside the kitchen. People were seated at the tables while others stood at the dispensers. He left and crossed the walkways until he stood in the center of the boulevard. He stared way up at the open skylight and the blue beyond. Somewhere within this gigantic cage of steel, plastic and humanity the tutu prowled.

"I'm coming," he murmured. "Wait for me and don't let anyone else bring you down. Your soul is reserved for me."

Corradado lay on the diving board and blinked in the sun. His back was warm, his belly full. He stretched to his entire length, ignoring the way the board creaked and dipped. If it broke and dumped him into the foul water he would tear it and the pool to pieces and go elsewhere.

His yellow eyes opened to stare at the corpse submerged in the reddening fluid, and for a few moments he was interested as the woman's open eyes looked straight up into his own. His muscles even tensed as he waited for her to exhibit some other sign of life. Then he relaxed. She might stare for eternity but never again would she make a voluntary mortal move.

The sun burned his back. For a moment he dozed. For an instant he was home again boring through solid rock with his baby claws. Condemned by his father to find his own living, he had chosen one of the mountains across the valley of molten lava, and into it he had gone like an ant into soil. Life was in the rock in the form of large burrowing animals called rakka; succulent, warm, nourishing, sufficiently difficult to catch so that Corradado, like most Flugers, remained thin and hungry. Unlike this planet, his homeworld was a place where food was hard to come by.

The partially eaten corpse in the pool yielded to gravity, rolled and turned so that the wound became visible where pelvis and legs had been consumed. Red seeped and spread below the Fluger like thick dye.

The pool room was at the bottom of the 0 which was third from the western end of Olympus, and it was therefore impossible for sunlight to pour in naturally, yet pour it did, as though the ceiling had captured its own solar body. In several places on the roof of the city were rectangular indentations lined with a special material called magnitum. A light repellent, it shunted sunrays onto lower shields that wound down, sideways, up or around into and through various parts of Olympus. A sun ray touched the topmost shield of magnitum and was shunted onto a lower one where it was again repelled and transferred to still another. The angles of the shields determined the direction in which the light flowed. It could wind like a corkscrew or travel at a slight angle. All sunlight in the city was crooked, save for that which came through open skylights or exterior windows.

Because the crooked light that flooded the pool room from a grille across the ceiling was hot and strong, Corradado nodded and indulged in daydreaming. One day when he was fully grown he would leave his mountain and go down into the deep caves of the valley, find a wife and take her back home. To her he would pledge to be civil, gentle, rational and reasonable, all those qualities he normally hated. She would make the same pledge to him. Their promises would extend to any children they might have.

That time wasn't now though. The big yellow creature on the creaking diving board wasn't fully grown and indeed was scarcely more than an adolescent, so all those things about

31

which he fantasized wouldn't be realities until some future date. In the meantime he was permitted by nature and circumstances to be his own explosive self.

The first thing Addard did when he awakened (as did several million other Olympians) was to switch on the *tev*, which took up most of the wall opposite his bed, and see what was new this morning.

What was new was plain for all to see, walking around in broad, crooked daylight, big and black, with the most ferocious features Addard had ever seen on any living thing. The sight of the animal was so startling that for a minute or two he lay in bed simply gaping.

All the intercoms in the apartment began jangling at once but he moved toward none of them. At some time today he would undoubtedly have to talk about the thing on the *tev*, so he might as well try to calm down and give it a critical look.

Four-legged, long-tailed, thick and muscular, serpentine in its litheness, the black creature was close to four meters in length and stood a meter and a quarter high. Its great muzzle was closed, for which fact Addard was grateful, as he didn't feel like seeing teeth at that moment. The beast was leisurely prowling through number eighteen park. Addard knew which park it was because he could see the gate and the number behind a row of shrubs. The *tev* cameras installed in trees by the weather people ground away and caught every movement made by the intruder. Naturally, there were no people in the vicinity.

Addard's astonishment changed to anxiety as it registered with finality in his mind that this animal was real and not a figment of his imagination, not a prank played by a cameraman, not anything other than some gross alien specimen casually wandering through a park in a city for which he was responsible.

The thing of it was that the intruder deliberately paraded before the cameras, or so it seemed, chose the most advantageous position from which it might be viewed. Back and forth it paced, occasionally turning, displaying its length, breadth and face, sleepy-eyed at first so that the mayor and the general populace didn't really get a glimpse of the two strange orbs through which it saw the world, but then the beast turned full-face to first one camera and then another. It snarled, showing long fangs, but more significantly it opened its eyes wide.

Addard shot straight up in bed and then leaned forward to get a better look, not that he needed one. He couldn't believe what he saw. He didn't think but simply stared into the ebon face with its fierce expression and threatening teeth. The eyes were a sparkling gray.

He dressed, bathed, carefully spread shaving cream on his face and neck and rinsed away his beard. The intercoms never ceased their jangling. While he put on his shoes he dialed for toast and cocoa on the wall dispenser beside his bed. He was one of the privileged few who wasn't forced to eat in a kitchen.

The black alien pictured on the *tev* screen had long since moved out of camera range and went away no one seemed to know where. Addard had already given the order for Kam Shar the Eldoron to be summoned to the meeting. A casual suggestion, such as, "Would Eldoron please report at nine o'clock," was going out on all public broadcasts, not interrupting programs or normal itineraries but imposing itself for the few seconds it took to be heard by the person for whom it was intended. People might wonder but it wouldn't upset them. How many of them had ever heard of the planet? A good guess on Addard's part might be six to a dozen out of the entire city. Space flight had been a reality for only a century, so relatively few planets had been studied or were even known of.

Ennesto walked into the office at five minutes before nine. He made a show of trying to move briskly but plainly felt all of his ninety-two years.

"You know it doesn't matter how old I am," he said, once he had joined Addard at the council table in the other's office. "I'm just as scared and worried as if I were forty like you."

Addard didn't reply. He wasn't certain it was a good idea for them to let down their hair before one another at this time. Olympians were undoubtedly doing that everywhere today, confessing their open and private fears to whoever would listen, but they probably didn't expect the members of their governing council to be doing the same.

33

Ennesto smiled as if he had caught an inkling of the mayor's disapproving thought. "Tranquilla was mayor when I was a young man. A very thoughtful fellow he was, considerate and as sensitive as an ascetic. There were plenty of aliens coming here for one reason or another, but he never let us see any who didn't look human." The old man raised a hand. "I'm not criticizing. It was all Varone's fault, jumping heedlessly into the mess in the first place, ordering an assassin the same way he'd order a pizza from a dispenser. Then he was sloppy and let the alien get away from the men he put to following him."

"Good morning," said Monkwell, striding in. His red hair was askew, his freckles dark and angry-looking against his raw skin. Garley trailed behind. It was exactly nine o'clock.

"I got in touch with Roxey," Garly said after seating himself. "Two large cartons and a trunk came off the spacer with Kam Shar. Roxey doesn't know where they went. He wasn't at the port for more than a few minutes. Being a roving foreman—"

"Yes, I know," said Addard. "He wouldn't normally be there, just as he wouldn't normally be around to see the Fluger disembark."

"He likes the ships." Pointedly looking about, Garly stroked his thin mustache. "I don't see our visitor from Eldoron."

"He could have smuggled the black animal inside one of the cartons," said Monkwell.

Garly shook his head and then shrugged. "I and my crew considered that, of course, so a while ago we checked the photographs taken of every item coming off the craft. The two cartons plus the trunk contained nothing living."

"Gas?" said Addard. "Possibly it was in the boxes and fooled the X rays."

"Can't be done," said Ennesto. "I worked in X ray for ten years and those machines can't be fooled. They can penetrate anything and pick up vital signs. If they say there was nothing alive in the alien's luggage, there wasn't."

"Could the technicians have been bribed?"

"Why does the black animal have to be connected with our assassin?" asked Monkwell. "Has anybody checked shipping lately to see if anything came in from space?"

"That's one of the first things I did after I was notified of

Varone's death," said Addard. "Nothing has come in since Kam Shar's transportation, and I've put a blanket on the landing port so that nothing else will be allowed in until I say so."

"No one and nothing in or out," said Garly. "We've checked and double-checked to account for everything. We have the Fluger and the Eldoron and we more or less know how or why they got here and we're reasonably certain they came by their lonesomes. So someone tell me what that thing was on the *tev* and how it got in number eighteen park."

They waited until eleven. "I have to go," said Ennesto.

They all had to go and each probably carried the same image in his mind as he went his separate way. Kam Shar. Alien. Assassin. He hadn't kept the appointment. He hadn't obeyed orders. None of them doubted the Eldoron had received the message about the meeting.

Chapter IV

For fracturing a man's skull, breaking his arm in two places and slicing off an ear the accused was tried in a court of law, found guilty of atrocious assault and battery and sentenced to five years.

He wept and his legs were too weak for him to walk so the guards had to help him along. Addard was reminded of an old film he had seen about a condemned man walking the last mile to the electric chair. The way this prisoner carried on one would think a place of execution awaited him at the bottom of the el. Not so, only a heavily guarded door.

The *tev* cameramen were not allowed in the el, only the prisoner, the two guards and Addard.

35

"I told them I was sorry!" the man gasped. His stark eyes were fastened on the city's leader. "You can help me! You can pardon me!"

"I can't. You know the law."

"I didn't mean to do it! Lock me up in a cell inside! Let me serve my term inside!"

The men carrying him stood him more or less on his feet, nodded to the others at the door. The prisoner screamed as it opened.

"I'll die out there! What'll I do? How will I live?"

The guards pitched him out of the city into the dirt and hideous open air of anarchy and independence. Scrambling erect, he launched himself at the entrance just as it slammed in his face.

Addard and the two court guards went back to the el, each absorbed in his own private turmoil. In exactly five years the man at the door would open it. If the prisoner was there he would be allowed back inside.

Addard's quarters were at the top of the third 0 where the larger, more expensive dwellings were situated. His office and living rooms were spacious with windows that seemed to open onto a sun-splashed blue sky. Corridors actually paralleled the exterior walls. Crooked light and one or two clouds super-imposed on a blue backdrop created the fresh effect. The mayor's office being the council room, it was very large and comfortably furnished.

His favorite white lounge was occupied by his number four adviser, which wasn't unusual at all, but when he saw who sat at ease beside her he came to a shocked halt.

The adviser got up, smiled at him and left the room without a word.

"I am here," said Kam Shar, remaining seated.

Swallowing his rage, Addard said, "You're late."

"I always choose my own times and usually my own places for meetings."

He was so cool, thought the mayor. Dressed all in black like a suave, sophisticated Lone Ranger. All he needed was a mask and smoking pistol. He carried no weapons, though, at least not in plain sight. Black trousers that fit perfectly, shirt of the same material, no pockets. It was the cloak that irritated

36

Addard, just a short black one that didn't flare or even move when Kam Shar arose or turned, not that the alien did either of those things now. He might have been glued to the lounge so motionlessly did he sit. Was his remaining seated a mark of disrespect?

"Exactly how much are you to be paid?"

"I've already been paid. It isn't logical to go on assignments without first banking the fee."

Not if you have a family, thought Addard. He wanted to ask but refrained. Somehow the idea of intimate conversation with this person offended him.

"Do you feel distressed?" Though his lips didn't move Kam Shar seemed to smile.

The mayor sat in the one place he could feel comfortable, in the head council chair. "Only because it's distressful to have a monster killing my people and to have a stranger from another world wandering about unescorted in my city."

The stranger from another world made no reply.

"You reside where in my city?"

Kam Shar merely looked at him with sparkling gray eyes.

"I can understand how you might prefer to remain independent but if I wish to contact you—"

"An announcement on the *tev* similar to the one you used to summon me this morning will be adequate."

"When you arrived on this planet you brought two large cartons and a trunk with you. Where are they? I realize you might be reluctant to answer so many questions, seeing as how our customs are bound to be different. You might even think I'm prying or threatening."

"It was understood before I accepted this assignment that there would be minimal contact with me."

"Then why did you come this morning, two hours late?" Addard kept his voice low and casual.

"Courtesy."

"Please understand that the man who hired you is dead and whatever information you or anyone else supplied him concerning your mission died with him. Surely you don't expect me to operate in the dark. I need to know more about you."

"I will do my work. Who, what and where I am is irrelevant."

37

"Not as long as you're in this city."

Kam Shar arose. "I must be about my business."

"What about those cartons you brought with you? What of the trunk?"

"What of them?" The alien moved to the open archway.

"I'm trying to be patient and reasonable," said Addard. "There surely is a common meeting ground between us where we can converse like civilized men. My city has paid you to do a job. Don't you feel any indebtedness to me?"

"No." Kam Shar went through the archway and was gone.

Addard couldn't believe it. He sat there for a minute or two listening and waiting for the Eldoron to come back into the room, expecting him with a feverish kind of anticipation. For the first time in his life he envisioned Olympus as a relatively small artifact perched on the shifting sands of the homeworld, vulnerable, unprotected against the unknown. What was that word? Tutu.

"I want the alien found," he growled into the intercom at his elbow.

"Which one?" said Monkwell, wide-eyed, alert, not meaning to be facetious or anything like it.

Addard spoke between his teeth. "Kam Shar. I don't want any reports about how hard you tried. You find out where he hangs his hat and where he stows his property."

"Okay," said the red-haired man and moved his hand as if to switch off his set.

"Am I finished?" said Addard.

"Sorry."

"Find the black alien too."

"What? Oh, the animal in the park. Why are you still calling it an alien?"

"To which earthly species do you think you can try to relate it?" said the mayor, and when Monkwell didn't answer he yelled, "Which one? Go on and tell me!"

After he got rid of his number three adviser he contacted Ennesto and Garly and told them the same thing, gave them similar orders. Then he sat and brooded. What was it like to have power over such a city? How many legions were at his command? He snorted. Never mind the ancient Romans, he had an army at his command if he wanted to use it. But against

38

what? A marauding animal or two and—maybe he shouldn't be thinking this but he would anyway—a hired alien who didn't know his place? Wasn't the police force at his beck and call and wouldn't every able-bodied man and woman in Olympus take up arms against a common foe, if need be? What was it like to have such power? He was beginning to find out and the discovery gave him indigestion.

"I expect you can float ten miles up if you want to," Quantro Tilzer said and secretly chortled up his sleeve. That old circus man had been right when he said there was a sucker born every minute.

The young man was sold hook, line and forty-seven dollars and all for just walking into the barber shop that Quantro would readily have admitted wasn't the best looking salon in Olympus. Wasn't the worst, either.

He didn't hear the young man's name and didn't care what it was, since he expected the other to come back time and time again. Eventually the name would be learned.

The patron sat in one of the big, plush swivel chairs, taking a spin or two as he gulped the laced cup of tea Quantro had handed him. The stuff would begin to melt as soon as it hit his stomach. Meanwhile, the establishment proprietor explained a few stupid eye exercises and some rituals the man was supposed to perform the moment he arrived home.

"You're sure you're going straight there?" asked Quantro, peering into the guileless eyes. What, he wondered, made young Olympians so gullible?

"Sure am. Straight home. Only been married two weeks. You think I'd stay away very long?"

Contrary to custom, Quantro never shaved and, just as contrary to custom, he was crooked, had nearly forgotten what it felt like to tell the truth. Now he pulled on his beard and pondered possibilities and ramifications. There was a chance that this sap might toot off in a cab, which would be fine for all concerned, since he would merely have a long, long jaunt around the city until the first effects wore off. Then again he might kill himself while doing something dangerous.

"You go straight to that little wife," he said, exhaling whisky breath into the cheerful face. "I'm telling you as a prospective astro that my routine has got to be adhered to right down to the dotted line."

Of course there was no dotted line in this situation, no forms or letters and certainly no signatures. He always sat in his salon until a sap walked in wanting to fly out of his body, at which time the barber sneaked a dope capsule into his or her tea, charged him or her a packet for the signs, exercises and rituals, and that was the end of it until the stuff wore off in a week or a month or however long it took, and then the customer came back.

"You going straight home?" he asked.

"Told you I was."

"You sound drunk to me."

"You smell drunk to me but I don't care 'cause I want to project, like I've seen in the films."

"Your wife know you're in here?"

The young man laughed. "She's the one sent me."

"Well, finish your tea and get out of here. I'm closing up."

"What, no haircut?"

The forty-seven dollars went into the safe behind the counter, after which Quantro dusted the eight plush chairs and the cutters attached to them, swept the floor and then checked his white locks in the long mirror that took up most of one wall. Deciding he disapproved of what he saw, he sat down in the nearest chair, fitted the cutting machine over his head and switched the dial to half a centimeter. The machine gripped his skull in a close embrace, the protected blades measuring each patch of his hair and taking off the exact amount. In three minutes a vacuum went on. When he pushed the cutter back and stood up, his hair was neat and trim and the debris had been disposed of in a bag beneath the machine.

Pressing the night button beside the archway, he stepped outside, locked his establishment by stepping on a round dial in the center of the threshold and started east along the nearest walkway. For a barber he was financially well off. His clothes were old and unattractive because he didn't care; he was clean because of his customers and he dealt in astro dope because he had no hobbies or morals.

Down the walkway he hurried, glancing back over his shoulder to make sure none of his rattled customers had picked

40

tonight to come and knock his block off. He didn't like violence. The mere thought of it turned his legs to water. In fact, he stumbled the very instant the idea of someone hurting him crossed his mind.

"What's the matter, fool?" he muttered, looking about to see if he had been overheard, but he was so alone on the walkway that his footsteps echoed and re-echoed from far off like ghostly twins. He had done it again, stayed in the shop too late and now he had to trek home with spirits. Infernally spooky they were tonight, skulking and sneaking and casting shadows everywhere.

Removing a flask from inside his shirt, he paused, raised it to his mouth and prepared to take a lusty swig. Instead he shrieked and stumbled backward, falling onto his rear but not releasing his hold on the liquor.

Dusting off the seat of his pants, he looked to see if anyone had witnessed his idiocy. No one had, and he finished what he had been in the act of doing before he hallucinated a giant beast leaping right over his head. Crazy, crazy. What kind of stuff was that to imagine when he didn't use his own merchandise?

His hand shook as he fastened the lid on the flask and returned it next to his ribs. He belched, spraying the air with bond. Then he laughed. It wasn't a pussy cat he had hallucinated, or a wolf, but it had to have been the biggest, toothiest son in existence. Good thing it didn't like the smell of eighty proof, otherwise it might have snatched his head off as it jumped twenty or thirty meters over him.

The thought made him snicker and then he snickered again, and so he wandered on home where it was lonely and dark and where the walkways were narrow, stingy and poorly constructed. Every now and then he belched, sometimes deliberately. Figment of his imagination or not, that son had been scary enough for him to ward it off like an evil spirit. Since it didn't like his whisky, he would saturate the air with it. A fella had to survive. Why? Quantro didn't know. The idea was just stuck up there in his mind like a postscript.

He had plenty of money but seldom spent any of it. His customers at the shop would have been surprised had they seen where he lived. People reserved the right to reside sumptuously or even meanly in Olympus and the latter best described Quantro's life-style when he wasn't at work. The neighborhood wasn't exactly dirty since garbage was always picked up by machines, but it wasn't exactly glowing either. The lights were weak, the air was of low quality and the apartments were minuscule and cheaply furnished.

He started to enter his front archway and tripped over the wooden cartons he had put out that morning. They were too big to fit into the disposal chute on the corner and the robot wouldn't be by until Tuesday. Quantro had planned to carry them out back to the pile when he came home from work.

Swearing, he gathered the crates into his arms and staggered around the building. Right away he wished he hadn't done it, right away he longed to be inside the apartment, maybe under the bed, or better yet a hundred kilometers away.

"Oh, sweetheart!" he gasped, lumbering about in the darkness as he attempted to regain his sense of direction. Was it possible one of his customers had turned the tables on him by fishing the dope capsule out of a cup of tea and dropping it into his? He let go of the crates and clawed at his throat, while somewhere ahead of him something huge and furtive moved across the pile of junk.

He was on his hands and knees then, crawling about as he tried to find the alley entrance. To the devil with the crates and he hoped they rotted, and speaking of the devil, he had that feeling again, as if the overgrown pup he had dreamed up was back again. Sweating profusely, he sat up, grabbed the flask from his shirt, yanked off the lid and sucked like a baby. To the devil with this devil, he would give it all the bad breath there was in the world.

Belching, gasping, blinking blindly, he crawled and blundered and finally found the alley opening. Hurriedly he unlocked his front archway by drumming his fingers in a specific sequence along the right side and tumbled inside.

Hulian searched for some kind of weapon to use against the yellow tutu. In a way it was too bad he had lost his sword, but then it had been too heavy to swing with any power, besides which he was in the city of pearls and ambrosia and would no doubt realize his every necessity and desire. When he finally met the tutu the appropriate weapon would be at hand, but in the meantime he intended to look around.

One misfortune of the day was that he had lost his way. Somewhere behind him was the boulevard with the statue of Jin Waken, whoever that was or had been, and he wanted to find it again before the night was over. One didn't sleep on benches or on the streets in Olympus. At midnight the cleaning machines came out with their scoops, brushes, sprayers, scrubbers and spears to make everything bright and sanitary and to chase everyone home.

The local map in Roxey's apartment had been of no use to him, while the general ones were too complicated, having too many words and confusing arrows, dots, stars, dashes, etc. He was, however, independent and used to taking care of himself, so he planned to investigate a little and if he didn't find anything he would go back and sound out Roxey. Probably that would be the wisest thing to do now, but he was restless and didn't like the cooped-up feeling the apartment gave him.

Being intelligent, he wasn't deceived when he saw the stars winking overhead, guessed they were either a mirror reflection directed downward from the roof like crooked light or a film. From somewhere came the hint of a night breeze. With it drifted the smell of lilac and rose. He tried to feel happy but he kept thinking of the person who had taken care of him for as long as he could remember. His earliest memories had the old man in them, holding his hand, teaching him, lecturing, warning, whipping, sometimes making him laugh.

This was the city of his innermost longings, the place of acceptance, the home where those of his species acknowledged that he was one of them. It was the abode of security and eternal progression. He sensed its mighty heartbeat, like a gigantic machine the oiled parts of which labored to maintain the humanity living within it.

As long as nobody saw his crazy blue eye he would fit in and be all right. But then perhaps people would consider that his brown eye was the crazy one. Both looked crazy to him when he looked in a mirror.

One day in his journeys he would locate the other tutu, the gentle one, and ask him to take out the blue eye and replace it with one the same color as his own. Maybe the tutu wouldn't be able to do it. Obviously he was like Roxey in that he couldn't distinguish between blue and brown. Then of course life wouldn't be impossible with eyes of a different shade. It might make conversation with girls easier to initiate. Conceivably they could like his looks.

He came to an exterior vestibule full of warning signs and lights, indicating that the balcony attached to it was the absolute end of the wing and there was nothing beyond it but empty air and space. During the day such areas were popular, no doubt serving as small cures for claustrophobics who believed they would never see the sky again. A high railing ran the length of the balcony, which was about ninety meters, and perched on the top near the center, his eyes stark and his hands nervously clutching the metal, was a young man.

"You're not going to jump!" Hulian said.

"Don't be silly. I'm going to fly."

"I don't think so. You don't have gray eyes."

"What does that mean?" The young man wasn't annoyed. He was in good spirits and laughed.

"If you aren't a gray-eyed tutu, you don't have wings, which means you can't fly."

"I'm talking about my spirit, dud! I'm an astro about to go into full flight in another minute or so, soon's the airy feeling gets better."

"You won't even make a splash down there, that's how high we are. More like a faint plop. Climb down off there."

The wind ripped through their hair and clothing, increased in velocity and gripped the young man as if with heavy hands. "Just a little more time!" he yelled. "I did the eye exercises and the rituals exactly like the barber told me. Another minute or so and I'll be light as air!"

"Get down!" yelled Hulian.

Leaning on the inside of the railing, the man said, "Stop worrying, you cockeyed freak, I'm out of my body. See it over there beside the wall?"

"There's nothing over there! You're doped up!" Hulian leaped and grabbed a foot. "Feel that? It's your body! The only one you have!"

"Whee! Light! Clear and free!" The man lost his grip on the rail and mashed his mouth against the metal as he fought for balance. Blood trailing down his chin, he straddled his perch and kicked at the boy. "I'm an astro! I'm out of my body! It was easy, just like skinning out of a sack!"

There was no one else near, nobody to call to for help, nothing for Hulian to do but fight the wind and cold, clamber up the framework of the railing and try to grab a foot or a portion of trousers. The man was out of his mind from whatever he had taken. His face white, bloody mouth sagging, eyes wide and burning with secret knowledge, he would fly on wings so gossamer they were nonexistent.

"My wife!" he croaked. "I should have gone straight home. She would want to do this with me." He kicked away the restraining hands, clambered upward until he was more or less standing in a bent crouch and away he plummeted into the endlessness of deadfall.

Chapter V

There were no children in most of the areas where Roxey worked. Sometimes he went to Eight, Nine or Ten to see some.

While he applied shaving cream to his face he thought about the orphan asleep on the couch in his living room. Correction: wetback. What was the difference and who cared? The kid had to have a place to stay; throwing him back to the outer slums made no sense. The conditions of his birth shouldn't have so much influence on his everyday life.

In the living room he took a final "look" at his boarder before leaving. Well-built kid, though a little on the thin side. Big hands and feet, like a puppy that still had growing to do.

There were a couple of teardrops on his cheeks, leftovers from waking or sleeping nightmares.

The temperature was a constant seventy degrees in the apartment, unlike section Two-K where his job awaited him. Giving the boy a last probe, he went into his office, descended a set of stairs to a tiny waiting station and stepped into the first cab that stopped. It took him to Three-L section and from there he rode swiftly to Two-G, met his crew and rode with them and the equipment to K in the same section.

K was full of snow, about two meters of it in some places, and it was still falling from the grille overhead. The machine was malfunctioning, which was why the maintenance crew had come.

Once upon a time, some restless soul had decided he was bored with a constant seventy degrees so he coerced his neighbors into clamoring for a weather change. From then on K was the place where it snowed indoors. Floors were replaced with screens that dumped the runoff into gutters, which took it to pipes where it was carried back to the snowmaker. Boulevards were knee-deep in white, walkways had to be shoveled every day, special departments stores with winter attire experienced thriving business, children were brought from their sections to see what fell outside from November to February, and if tenants got sick of K they could make arrangements to exchange living quarters with someone in another section.

The ceiling of the main boulevard was high enough so that it was obscured whenever snow fell. It was not a great height, and Roxey was riding an el up a wall when he heard screams coming from below. Normally work crews approached their task from above, traveling in ceiling els beyond public view, but it was sometimes faster simply to climb to the construction site in one of the mechanical cages hanging on most of the walls of the city. All the crew had to do was clean the big filter in the snow machine, hack away a little accumulated ice, perhaps replace a power pak.

Roxey was about ten meters up the wall when he heard the yelling. Stopping the lift, he leaned over a rail and immediately saw what was causing the havoc. It was the same creature that had come leaping and growling out of the hold of the spacecraft that day not long ago. It was the UKO, the Unidentified Killing Object.

His mechanical eyes worked at top speed, sending him a myriad of strong or weak, long or brief signals so that he knew exactly what was happening.

Corradado came prowling along number six walk at his leisure, seeming to find the snow interesting. Now and then he stopped to taste it. He sank down into the stuff until his legs and underbelly were hidden.

Eventually everyone saw him, but at first only a few knew he was there. Having seen the black alien on the *tev*, most of the populace believed that had been the UKO, although those who saw Corradado knew right away that he was a thing to be avoided or gotten away from.

The man nearest the yellow creature dropped his packages and plunged into the snow, only to lose his footing. Instead of bounding after him, Corradado bored through the white mounds, ducked his head and pulled the man all the way under.

Most people didn't run. Either they were stricken with mind stall or realized that moving targets attracted attention. It didn't matter which course of action or inaction they chose, for the Fluger seemed intent upon greeting them all, plowing or bounding, boring or crawling and then swiping at them with devastating paws.

Policemen rushed from a department store to take careful aim with their weapons. Only Roxey was able to follow the flight of the projectiles and only he could say why they did no damage. As soon as he picked up the officers and realized they were going to shoot, he switched the unit in his pocket to slow motion. The signals came to him as if from deep water, steady and readable.

Corradado's skin wasn't particularly thick but it was so tough and pliable that it could repel invasion at an instant's notice. Or even quicker. The first bullet started to hit him in the right flank as he leaped into the air to come down on a woman. Tracing the outline of the flesh on the yellow body, the slug turned and made a faint mark before ricocheting away into the snow. The second bullet struck a portion of his back. The portion immediately sank inward so that the metal tip was diverted, and away the object went into a white mound.

47

Whether the shots caused Corradado any pain at all remained a mystery to Roxey, who clung to the el and viewed the scene in his extraordinary manner. All the while, he hoped and waited for the alien to be brought down. There was too much noise, too much bedlam, too much panic and no planning or anticipating. The more the policemen fired their guns the closer they moved to the target. That was a mistake because the Fluger almost literally shoved their weapons down their throats.

Those who made it inside the stores remained safe; after having cleared the boulevard of shrieking impediments, the creature moved on and disappeared through the arched exit into section L. Behind he left a quiet boulevard of snow and torn bodies. Roxey had seen all of it except for the technicolor effect; white on red, red on white, bubbling, running, at last still.

The *tev* news programs cautioned people not to give way to hysteria. They were intelligent and civilized and there was no need to tell them the UKO would be destroyed. The police force in every section was on full standby alert. The army was setting up small-weapons arsenals, and guard units were stationed at every boulevard. Not only the main byways were being staffed but also other streets, cab tunnels and maintenance areas. It would take a while to catch the Fluger. Yes, that's what it was. No, it wasn't an ordinary animal or even an unordinary one. Yes, from another planet. No, not from Earth but from a different world. You see, it was this way. . . .

Ennesto's trial force tracked the Fluger to park number sixty-eight. While he was bursting in through the huge western archway, they burst in through the eastern one, three little helicopter fighters with a full complement of armaments.

Most Olympians carried tiny *tevs* in their pockets so that at any given time they could find out what was going on in their metropolitan world by simply pulling out the antenna and channeling a news report. The visitors in the park had gotten the word that the UKO was headed their way and hastily vacated the premises, all except three equestriennes, one of whom was unfortunate enough to rein her mount directly toward the western arch. The other two galloped away to safety.

Corradado had never seen a horse before but seemed to know how to handle one. Standing upright and with a forward and downward thrust of his left rear paw, he partially disemboweled the animal, plucked the rider from its back and pulled her to pieces.

Pilot two arrived on the scene in time to drop a fireball that fell like a bag of sand onto the thrashing horse. Sparks and hurtling flame hit the Fluger. Pilot two didn't believe the UKO could jump so high but that didn't stop Corradado from springing ten meters straight up in the air. He slapped the little fighting machine in the side so hard that it went reeling like a crippled bird. Its propeller stopped, the craft turned on its back and fell. By the time it exploded Corradado was after another machine and pilot number one.

It hadn't taken more than a glance for number one to know what had happened to his comrade. It was with grim intent that he pursued the UKO into thickly wooded areas of the park. He flew back and forth over the trees trying to spot the target, when all at once he was frightened nearly out of his wits by the creature hurtling up at him. Corradado had climbed one of the tallest trees and then leaped. Although he fell short of number one flying craft, the pilot was unnerved sufficiently to behave irrationally.

Just ahead of machine-gun bullets sped the alien, the slugs making twin furrows in the grass behind him. Meanwhile number three vehicle tried to catch him in a crossfire. The pilots abandoned this tactic when they nearly collided, paralleled one another and ran the enemy into the woods again. Pilot one likely suffered feelings of shame and revenge-lust, for when his gun ran out of ammo he dropped fireballs onto the UKO. The flames had no more effect on the yellow creature than the bullets.

Pilot three had been yelling into his radio for one to stop using the fireballs while he was over the woods, but one seemed to think he had a good thing going and zoomed after the Fluger like a Zero. A few of the trees began to burn. Then the brush caught fire.

The target was obscured by the billowing smoke. Meanwhiie, the pilots had to go on automatic because there was suddenly nothing but great volumes of gray clouds around them. The smell of burning leaves and timber permeated the air.

The park's air-conditioning worked at full capacity for a while before signaling for Fire Control, which was another mechanical system. Eventually Automatic Radar Control in both flying ships signaled a solid mass in every direction. The systems turned themselves off by switching to hover, two meters above the ground for one and two meters from the park's eastern wall for three.

Untrammeled by the poor vision of humans, Corradado saw quite well in and through the smoke. He spied the hovering one and leaped on it as he had once leaped on one of Olympus' finest tanks, bit the propeller in half, simultaneously crushed the cab shield and pilot, turned and cow-kicked the craft into shards of glass and bent metal.

Pilot three didn't know where he was. Blinded by smoke, beginning to suffocate, he decided to creep upward and find cleaner air. His propeller clipped an outcropping of plastic and mortar protruding above the eastern archway, broke and dropped off. After that the fighter fell and created its own fireball.

Fire Control sent probes into the atmosphere and immediately dumped tons of water on the park. The ventilation systems were overloaded and the smell of the fire penetrated into several other sections of the city, where some people panicked and created minor incidents.

Otherwise, life went on as before. A horse, a woman and three pilots were dead, three vehicles were pulp, park sixty-eight was ruined, the UKO was still at large. Ennesto's coup hadn't come off.

"You won't be able to kill him, boy," Roxey said to Hulian. They sat in the living room watching the *tev*. It took up one entire wall. "I know a little bit about how that alien operates and I'm telling you to leave him to the experts."

"According to the newscasts they aren't doing so well."

The foreman had a one-track mind when he wanted. "Besides which, you have to think about staying out of sight of anybody with any authority, and practically everyone has some. If your eyes are as noticeably different as you say, they'll get you and toss your carcass out the front door along with the criminals."

"You don't understand," said Hulian.

"Sure I do. You want to get even for your old friend, who sounds like he was the proper fellow to raise you."

"That thing took out my eye!"

"And you want revenge for that too. Well, as far as that goes, I expect there are thousands of Olympians with good cause to want some revenge on that big son. He's only killed about seven hundred people so far and destroyed property to the tune of a billion dollars. What I'm trying to say is, if you want to get your licks in you'd better get in line."

"Whoever gets there first is the one who'll count."

"Not necessarily. In a manner of speaking I've seen more than one person get to him first, but he just made hamburger out of them as fast as he did the ones who came later."

"You don't understand. You got no eyes. What do you know?"

"That you're lonely and in need."

Hulian frowned and then sighed. "You're not supposed to spell it out like that. You can say I don't mind company, or something like that, but anything plainer is embarrassing. I'm not three years old, you know."

"You like the new boots I got you?"

"Yeah, fine. I never had anything like them. In fact, I never had anything period." Hulian never asked the blind man why he let him stay, why he didn't throw him out. He didn't have to. Every time he looked at the ugly face and the slate-blue dead eyes he could feel the gentleness and affection emanating from the big man. "You don't have to worry," he went on. "Revenge only takes a moment and then I'll have a lot of time to read your books like you want me to and learn how to work with you."

"Revenge is like justice, kid. Sooner or later it has its own way, and time is meaningless."

"Still, you don't mind if I go out on my own once in a while? I mean, I have to be free."

"And if you don't come back one day I'll just know you're

either dead or you got thrown out on your ear and then I'll forget I ever knew you."

"Whatever happens, you're not to worry. But if I can, I'll come back."

They didn't have too many conversations like that. Usually they talked about the economy and politics and how various factions within the city vied for attention by lobbying or advertising in the media, or both. For instance, some groups advocated letting all the slum people in as citizens, while other groups deplored the idea and said it would mean overpopulation and a subculture whose detrimental influence would be immediate.

Slow but steady absorption of slummers was suggested by yet other groups, and this policy was in fact being carried out nearly every day and had been for decades. The descendants of malcontents and criminals, the slummers had never been forgotten by most of Olympus. The fact that a fair number of them lived in the shantytowns outside secure walls was due to intellectual snobs and political neurotics, who insisted that the quotas remain small.

"Maybe when you grow up you'll want to be a lawyer or a politician," Roxey said to Hulian.

"Maybe. Funny how I keep thinking about aliens and other worlds."

"You better quit it. Only people who don't want a home or country have anything to do with outer travel. And they're bound not to like us out there."

"Why?"

"We're too opinionated, too ready to argue points."

"Tutu is always fascinating, though." Hulian didn't say anything about the flying man with gray eyes. He had already told all he knew. Roxey thought he made it up.

As if reading his mind, the big man said, "I've been thinking about that alien you told me about, the one you think gave you your new eye. To fix a wound like that and implant a whole new one would take the medical knowledge of a specialist."

"He's color-blind. That's the only thing he doesn't know about doctoring."

"He'd have to have used one of our clinics. Now, just tell me he marched or flew into one and asked the staff to scram."

"I was half conscious so how do I know?"

Roxey shook his head. There were three eye banks in the city and he had visited each of them. The fact was that they didn't do a great deal of business that wasn't on an appointment basis, so most of the time they were unstaffed and closed. The duty people couldn't tell him if anyone had been using any of the offices illegally and they didn't know if a blue eye was missing since they had so many eyes and eye parts they couldn't keep track of them all. If it weren't for the kid being so explicit about how the Fluger had come running across the ground outside and ripped out his eye, Roxey would be convinced the flying alien was born of a nightmare.

"That Fluger can't be killed," he said.

"Not even in this city?"

"Tell me how. Bullets won't penetrate his skin and fire doesn't faze him."

"Why don't they drown him?" Though he asked the question, Hulian wasn't interested in the answer. He felt secure in the knowledge that nobody but him could hurt the Fluger. He owed old yellowhide. It was that simple.

Corradado lay on the pile of junk behind Quantro Tilzer's quarters and yawned into the darkness. He hadn't slept for a long time. Still, he wasn't exhausted. He wouldn't be ready for the real sleep for a while. On occasion he napped for a minute or two but his brain didn't allow its upper levels to shut down. There were too many stimulants being carried there by his blood, although after a period of time the stimulants would cease to be produced and his brain would experience a change. He would sleep an almost dead sleep for seven solid days.

Now he yawned and dreamed of the home mountain. Momentarily his jaws ached with longing for the sweet, crisp taste of rakka. Secretly he grinned. He didn't want to go home. Not being old enough for a wife, there was nothing for him to do on Fluga but bore through rock like a big mole. There were no shrieking, two-legged animals on the homeworld. This was a shame since they were entertaining as well as nourishing, not as large as rakka but far more courageous and original.

Never would a rakka build a metal contraption and try to defend itself against a fluger.

Tensing, the big creature peered through the gloom, watched as the stinking shrieker staggered down the alley. Every night this same item who smelled so bad came to the pile to add something to it. Corradado knew that the reason the other came was to see if he was really there. No doubt, the inferior mind believed or hoped there was a large rat or other vermin playing in his pile. The alien lashed out with his tail and sent a few crates rocketing to the ground. This made the shrieker cry out and fumble for his flask. Afterward he sprayed the air with the peculiar stink, which was why instead of springing for the scrawny throat, Corradado lay back and rumbled low in his throat.

He didn't hate the smell of whisky that much. The truth was he never retreated to the dark alley until he was tired and had eaten his fill. But the stink was no good. His low estimation of shriekers fell even lower. Though they didn't taste bad, they had bad taste.

The inferior life form went back where he had come from, and the creature lay among the crates and other trash and rested. Listening, feeling the faint pulsations of the thousand and one engines below the street, he decided that being in this foreign place was like being in a rock cavern beneath a great waterfall. Both were closed in and gave him a tight sensation just thinking about them.

Had he been at home when such feelings visited him, he would have clawed his way to the surface to get to openness. Perhaps it was storming at home now, with crackling thunder making the mountain shudder while the lightning bolts licked the ground like fiery tongues. There had been occasions when a bright flash was attracted to Corradado and had actually struck him, but it couldn't hurt him. Interwoven within the layers of his tough skin was a natural mesh-like conductor that prevented the electricity from doing him any damage. Were Flugers not provided by nature with the mesh, the lightning would have killed them all long ago.

Chapter VI

Roxey sometimes forgot that others could see, so when he received orders from Garly he wrote them on a Braille screen, intending to refer to them in the morning. The screen had a surface so soft and liquid-like that he could fingerpaint words and symbols that raised and hardened for him to read later. He forgot the screen would be visible to Hulian.

The boy hadn't wasted a minute of his time, studied old newscasts on *tev* tapes, looked at photographs in bound books and microfilmed volumes, learned how to decipher maps, etc. When he discovered Roxey was going to be part of a ploy to catch the UKO, he also discovered that the action would take place in 3-Y-4-(2). By then he was sufficiently skilled to locate the area on a map and find it by traveling in cabs.

3-Y-4-(2) was an artificial lake surrounded by a sandy beach laid on top of a soft floor. Paralleling the beach was rich sod, upon which grew Kentucky bluegrass. Palm trees jutted from buried pots, as did cherry and maple trees and a variety of flowers.

Just inside the western archway several large chunks of raw beef lay dehydrating in the crooked light of the sun. They had been dipped in a tasteless, virulent poison. Half a kilometer east a large dog strained at a leash that kept it secured to a cherry tree. Buried in the flesh of its right flank was a capsule of poison.

Here and there were narrow strands of wire that came from the sand and stretched toward the sky, seeming to go nowhere and to serve no purpose. They were the only visible parts of a net lying beneath the sand of the beach to the right of the lake and just beyond the dog.

Clouds of porous material oozing billowing vapor had been hung low in the overhead to camouflage groups of men working on platforms.

Garly's plan was for the Fluger, who was heading their way, to eat one of the poisoned chunks of meat and promptly drop dead. In case he only liked living food—and so far that seemed to be his distinct preference—he would proceed to the dog, eat it and then drop dead.

In the event that he ate no poison at all, he would still have to travel on the south side of the lake (if he was in a lazy mood and didn't feel like making his own passageway), since the north side had been blocked off near the west entrance. The plan was for him to walk in all the right places, be lifted into the air by the net and dumped into the lake, which was carrying a charge of electricity strong enough to sizzle the horn off a rhino.

It was all for nothing, though, and if Garly hadn't had license to use the taxpayers' money as he saw fit, dimly or lucidly, he would have been hauled forward and reprimanded. However, nobody knew but the crews who had instigated the action. Corradado came roaring through the western archway in fine fettle, having just done a million dollars' damage in a residential area. He immediately went over to a chunk of meat and sniffed it. Passing on by, he sniffed another chunk and then another. None interested him.

His attention was soon attracted by the dog. He pounced on it, decapitating it with one bite. He didn't swallow the head but spat it out before tearing the carcass to pieces. He ate none of it. Rumbling in his throat, glaring about, he prowled forward a few paces and then sprang backward as the net darted up out of the sand and closed on him. If the lake hadn't been so near he would have walked away free, for swipes from his claws parted the heavy metal mesh like cobwebs.

The crane manipulating the net was fast and dumped him into the water before he was all the way out of the trap. While the men on the platforms began congratulating each other, he sank to the bottom of the lake, walked along the bottom and climbed out. The electricity hadn't harmed a hair of him.

He surprised everyone by disdaining to exit via the eastern

archway, choosing instead to use his claws to tear a hole in the wall.

The only one who followed him through the opening and saw which way he went was Hulian. Dropping from the palm tree in which he had been hiding, the boy slipped through the jagged aperture in time to see Corradado's rear quarters disappear into a wide cab tunnel.

There were lights for a while but then they faded, and soon he walked in utter darkness. Here was a graveyard for machines in a state of needing repairs. The large enclosure in which he finally found himself might have been endless for all he could tell. Somewhere on a wall a revolving blue light flickered on and off. It was a monitor that read the temperature, atmosphere and weight of the room and its contents. Infrequently the blue light glanced upward into dim reaches.

Hulian gradually began to regret having followed the Fluger from the lake. He was in a metal cemetery with the enemy, weaponless and as blind as Roxey without his radar gear.

Quietly reaching out to a stalled floor sweeper, he began climbing as quietly as he could, listening for the faint growls the Fluger made somewhere to his left. There would be no heroic confrontation today nor, he hoped, a cowardly or terrified one either. He must climb, get away from the danger, not make any noise lest the burrowing blitz paint the dead machines with his blood.

He knew he was very high now, perhaps as much as fifteen meters. There must have been trapdoors or els built into the ceiling through which the machines were lowered or picked up. He didn't recognize the contours of the thing upon which he rested, but it was long and narrow like a cab tunnel tie.

As he instinctively scooted away from the growling sounds, the shape of the metal rail under him suddenly became narrower and, to his horror, tipped slightly and emitted a piercing squeal. At once the growls coming from below ceased, and almost as quickly he heard Corradado climbing up toward him.

Thoughts of revenge dropped from his mind faster than the perspiration coursed down his neck. Ever so cautiously he scooted farther along the rail, at the same time reaching and probing as high as he could to find something else upon which to climb. He touched a solid platform, immediately scrambled onto it and knew a certain satisfaction when the rail fell and hit the Fluger.

Now he was motionless, crouched upon the landing, listening as keenly as he had ever done, while Corradado paused to complain about the thing that had struck him. It was quiet in the graveyard's heights, black, oily-smelling, dusty and totally still except for a single sound. Someone breathed almost directly behind him. Scant little sucking noises, in and out, in and out, came from just over his left shoulder.

Panic could take over in moments like this. Hulian didn't scream or throw himself onto the machines but slowly turned his head to see what was behind him. Not yet was it time to yield to fate or the Fluger. Not quite yet.

Even as he turned to look, the blue light on the far wall threw a feeble beam his way, shone directly onto a face partially obscured by darkness. Only the startling gray eyes were visible.

Conscious of the chill sweat soaking his clothes, he held back a sob of relief, quietly moved along the platform and stopped close to the shining eyes. Tutu. Friend. Giver of a blue eye. Winged savior.

"Help me get out of here so I can kill him later," he whispered.

There was no reply, no reaction, nothing at all. The weird eyes glittered and Hulian relaxed and waited to see how long it would take for the Fluger to decide between continuing to climb and going away.

Danger was too close. Fear still tightened his throat. Because the gray eyes were only slightly above his head, he assumed the tutu was also sitting. Fondly he raised a hand and laid it on what he expected to be a man's shoulder. Or perhaps a wing. But then, no, he must have imagined the flying while he was still feverish. Was not the tutu a man?

His hand sank into crisp, thick fur. Startled, he could only turn his head and meet the gray eyes staring into his own. Yes, they were much too far apart for a man's, an item he ought to have noticed right away. Whatever it might be that he had his hand buried in, it wasn't the feathers or hair of a man, winged or otherwise. It was an animal.

With a flash of insight he knew it was the black beast he had seen on the *tev* a few weeks ago. Yet the gray eyes were the same. There was but one thing to do—sit motionlessly and see if the black one attacked him. Better to be killed by gray eyes than the yellow monstrosity below.

The beast didn't make a sound, moved not a millimeter. Hulian began breathing again, even let his hand fall away from the thick ruff. They sat in blackness while Corradado gave off growling and climbed in earnest up the machines. With each grunt he drew closer, causing the boy to press back instinctively against the animal. It wasn't there!

Now beginning to panic, he reached for it, sighed with relief when he felt it a little distance away. He touched its tail and it retreated, but it waited for him and moved a bit more when he touched it again.

With Corradado behind him he crawled forward, raised up and climbed onto the broad back of the tutu just as it leaped into what seemed to be empty air. They landed on something else, and the tutu leaped again, landed and leaped, all without making more than a whisper of sound. Hulian had his arms around the powerful neck and his face buried in the ruff. Gulping away his fear he clung with love, need and gratitude.

They left the metal graveyard and entered a series of smaller, darker compartments—or at least that was what they seemed to be. It was almost immediately obvious to him that the black tutu had excellent night vision, for he skipped up stairs, down inclines, through archways and across floors with rapidity and no hesitation. All the while Corradado traced their every step, perhaps not as quickly but just as surely. It appeared to be only a matter of time before he bridged the distance between them.

They entered a room with an odor like none other Hulian had ever smelled. He clung tightly to the furry neck while the tutu made a high leap and started climbing, landing and then leaping broadly, and so forth until finally he paused. There came a low whirring sound from somewhere in the darkness. Hulian held his breath as he felt his mount bunch its muscles and prepare for a special jump. They leaped, landed and then slowly began revolving around and around. For a while, the tutu stood quietly as if he were catching his second wind. The final jump was almost straight up. Afterward the animal sprawled flat in exhaustion and breathed heavily. The boy slipped from its back, lay beside it, very soon falling asleep.

Just after the crooked light of dawn was diverted down through the building into the room, he awoke and immediately saw Corradado hunched on a narrow ledge below them, eyes half closed as he contemplated the large fan in the center of the ceiling. It spun at such a rapid rate now that its four blades were invisible. Hulian knew that last night the thing had scarcely moved. Of course it was powered by light and now went so fast the Fluger couldn't leap onto one of the blades and follow the enemy into the niche in the corner of the ceiling. He hadn't jumped onto the fan during the night because he couldn't see well enough in the dark.

Hulian lay in the cubbyhole with his head over the edge and watched the yellow alien, stared down into its mad eyes and wondered if it saw as he saw, thought as he thought, hated as he and his kind hated.

"I was afraid of you last night, but never again," he said softly. "Now I know you have weaknesses."

The room was a spacious gymnasium redolent with the aftereffects of sweat socks and resin. There was a boxing ring near the western archway; beside it a trampoline and parallel bars. There were rings, mats, punching bags, nets, enough equipment and space for a dozen sports to be simultaneously played. Along the north and south walls were graded steps running nearly to the ceiling, two meters apart, ornamental and never intended for climbing.

Hulian looked over his shoulder at the black beast. That was when he saw the man propped against the wall in the back. He looked dead, which Hulian thought was too bad because he bore a strong resemblance to the winged tutu who had saved his life. He remembered that he now owed a debt to two strange ones.

For a while Corradado squatted on the last carved step, which was some four meters lower than the fan. He could easily have made the leap were it not for the speed of the blades. If he waited for the light to fail tonight, the blades would come to a near stop, but he might aim badly and miss the intended one in the darkness. It was a long way to the floor. Not that he feared such a fall would hurt him, but it might draw the attention of shriekers, who would have cause to rejoice at his chagrin.

The thought made the yellow one snort. No matter. Of what use was it to stay here on this tiny ledge and hope the fan broke down so he could get to the hated black enemy and the puny shrieker? It was time to leave this stinking room and return to his refuge for a brief rest. He and the ebon hero would meet again.

The Fluger had long been gone by the time Hulian crawled to the back of the niche, squeezing past the black beast, to examine the man for wounds.

"He's dead," he said to the animal. It lay on its stomach snoring. At his words it opened its gray eyes and then closed them again.

The man was dressed in a plain black blouse and black trousers. "He feels warm," Hulian said. "Maybe he isn't dead." It occurred to him that the man might have died while he slept. Didn't a body retain its heat for a while? The corpse's face wasn't pale. Its lips were pink like the winged tutu's.

"What has happened to the world between now and the time of all those things the old man told me about?" he asked. He expected no response from the black one and received none. "The old man cared for me after my mother died. I don't remember her. He told me the way things were and he mentioned every living creature he could remember, but not once did he ever talk about you or anything like you." Thoughtfully he looked at his companion. Its eyes were closed but he knew it wasn't sleeping. "Neither is there supposed to be such an animal as the yellow murderer. It seems that the sky has begun to rain more than dogs and cats."

Patting the man's cheeks, he tried to revive him. "He's dead but he isn't dead," he said. "Another mystery. A single one is easy to handle but I'm getting too many."

One thing he knew was that he wasn't afraid of the black tutu. Still tired and willing to wait for the other to get him out of the niche to safety, he lay down and threw his arm across the furry neck. It was in that exact instant that he felt the life go out of the animal, all at once, snuffed like a candle, living and strong one instant and flaccid the next.

He didn't believe it and shook the black head, making it loll. Frightened, he pressed his back against the wall. It had died for no reason and practically before his eyes. He stuck out his foot, nudged it in the ribs. So much lifeless meat. He was trapped up here with two corpses. Except that one of them wasn't really dead.

After examining the animal with care he decided it wasn't really dead either. Only the capacity for action had gone out of it. Forlorn, miserable, he sat and thought of the unreason of his recent life.

A short time passed and then he heard a familiar sound. The beating of wings interrupted his reverie and he hurriedly crawled to the mouth of the cubbyhole at the same moment that the winged tutu of his feverish dream appeared in the air. It was the very same person. In fact, it looked a great deal like the dead man and even the black beast. There were the eyes and the lips, and this one's curly dark hair was like the animal's fur.

Hulian stepped back when the other gestured for him to do so. The wings flapped mightily and loudly as the tutu told him what to do. He gripped the dead man's legs and hauled the body to the opening. The tutu picked up the limp form and flew away with it, crossed the room near the ceiling, stepped onto an outcropping of tile and crawled through a vent.

He was back in about ten minutes. "Hurry," he said, hovering just outside the cavity. "I must be back and concealed before the athletes come for morning practice." He stretched out his arms and Hulian stepped into them, clamped his legs around the slender thighs and his arms around the strong neck.

Beyond the vent was a spacious tunnel some ninety meters long, which the tutu climbed through. Then it went through another opening and began to fly. The wind whipped through Hulian's hair and clothing. When he dared to look down he saw nothing but white clouds. Then, turning his head, he had a bird's-eye view of Olympus, which looked like a city of heaven or a fort straight from mythology, rising invincibly above the clouds, all pastels and glittering glass. It didn't look real.

Flying over the city, the winged man dropped to a ledge outside a window. Within was an office room and on the couch slumped the body of the man who had been in the niche only minutes before.

The winged one didn't go inside with Hulian but waited until he was safely deposited upon the floor before flying away. Not having received any instructions, the boy knew he was to stay where he was, at least for the time being. There was no one in the bedroom or living room of the apartment, which was so large and luxurious that he realized it belonged to someone important. But not overly important. Were there not people in Olympus who made mere mortals appear quite common?

He was in the act of patting the cheeks of the corpse when its two sparkling gray eyes opened and looked at him. Two hands took his own.

"Don't cry out," said Kam Shar.

"I won't. A little thing like this couldn't make me yell."

The alien smiled. "Go now. I'll wait here for an appointment."

"Can't I be with you?"

"We'll meet again, I promise."

"Thank you for the eye. I didn't have a chance to say it to the one with wings but I have an idea any of the three would do."

"Don't get trapped by the Fluger. He has marked you for his own. Hurry and lose yourself in the crowd on the walks."

"You can understand my position, I believe," said Addard. "In the first place our outercom system is new within this century so that our sense of protocol isn't as established as it might be. In other words, if we offend people from other worlds it isn't intentional."

Kam Shar wasn't seated, another point that irritated the mayor. The Eldoron didn't seem to want to sit down, preferring to tower over him. He didn't say much, either.

"You can understand my position." Addard frowned. He had already said that. "One of my subordinates hired you," he went on. "A man named Varone. Dead, you know. He didn't understand a great deal about the ramifications of bringing an alien into the country. The world. Someone he knew nothing about."

Kam Shar stood wordlessly, attentively.

"You're fired," said Addard.

His words elicited no reaction from the offworlder.

"Go back where you came from." Addard grew angrier as he realized he wasn't carrying the conversation the way he had intended. For some reason the words weren't coming out of him the way he had rehearsed them. "I don't wish to insult, offend or wound," he said. "I'm responsible for the thirty million people in this city. There isn't anyone else I can point to in the event of fiasco or disaster. I want you to take the things you brought with you and go to the spaceport where the same ship is waiting to take you aboard."

Still Kam Shar said nothing.

"Didn't you hear me? We want you to leave Earth and return to Eldoron or wherever you want to go, as long as it's off our planet."

"I haven't done what I came to do." Kam Shar's voice was casual. The words came easily. Unlike Addard, he wasn't disturbed.

"We'll take care of the Fluger. You can keep the money."

"I must hasten and finish my plans to destroy the invader."

"You obviously fail to comprehend what I've been saying to you. Your job here is finished. We don't want you to stay. You're to go to the spaceport and fly out of here. Surely you don't insist upon staying where you aren't welcome?"

"Soon," said Kam Shar. "It won't take long and then he will be destroyed." While Addard looked after him in pain, rage, anguish and a variety of other emotions, he walked out of the apartment.

Addard slumped in his chair and massaged the back of his head which felt as if it might be splitting. What was he to do? Would his advisers or anyone else take him seriously if he told them how impossible it was to talk to the man? Alien. Incredibly different.

Randecker had filled him in early that morning: "At birth they come with three bodies, not just one like us. Three tiny little forms, one humanoid, one with wings and a black, four-legged thing that looks like a cross between a wolf and a bear. We've all seen that one on the *tev*. Only the humanoid body mates; the other two are sterile. But they can transfer their mind or their soul or their essence, whatever you want to call it, into any of the three bodies at will. While they're in one form the other two are in suspension, not dead but not really alive. It's as if they leave a spark of themselves in two bodies while they fully inhabit the third.

"It takes them about fifty of our years to mature, so their

life-spans are two to three times longer than our own. They're intelligent and dedicated to their work, so much so that it won't do you any good to try to get rid of yours before he finishes his job. If you're thinking about it, forget it. He doesn't know the meaning of failure or futility.

"That's all I know right now, boss. Don't ask me to elaborate on or explain anything I've told you because those people at the research station on Lambda didn't give me anything but those few facts. Neat, eh? Good luck. Oh, one more thing. They emphasized this: don't make him angry, whatever you do, or he'll bring your city down around your ears. Those are their exact words. I won't try to explain them either."

Latest *tev* newscast: "Indictments will shortly be handed down for at least two prominent scientists. Three test-tube experiments at the lab in Section Four, Level Nine got out of hand six months to a year ago when the three experimental subjects not only were not destroyed in the making or soon thereafter but were allowed to grow, mature and then escape. They are in the city now, those three subjects, and Olympians are alerted. . . ."

Chapter VII

For a long time Addard sat staring into space. He was thinking of nothing at all. His mind was curiously blank, as it had been so often of late. By and by his hand went out to the intercom on his desk and automatically he punched out the code for the red line to the mayor of Superior. Locked. Wendelar still wasn't answering calls. He should have gone to her with his hand out a month ago.

Coming to a decision, he hurriedly arose, passed through the narrow archway in the southwestern corner of the room, ran down the steps to the station and pressed a red button on the wall. From somewhere in the myriad tunnels eastward a sleek cab wheeled from a storage room and entered its private track. In a few moments it stopped for its passenger, after which it embarked upon a course that carried it down a gradual decline to Earth's ground level. Not pausing there, it continued going deeper until it was two hundred meters below surface. Then it sped at thousands of kilometers an hour, finally slowing and eventually stopping when an obstacle ahead made its presence known on the guidance and radar systems.

For a minute or two Addard thought the obstacle might be the Fluger. By the time he drew near enough to see what it was he was bathed in perspiration brought about first by terror and then rage.

This time when he punched out Wendelar's code on the intercom in the cab she answered personally.

"There's a barricade across the track."

"My apologies," said the mayor of Superior. "It's there to keep you from coming any closer. We've barricaded all the tracks."

"When?"

"Within the last hours."

"This is stupid!" he exploded, hating her serenity. She could afford to be calm since she was on the right side of the concrete wall she had placed in front of the cab, while he was on the wrong side. "The creature wouldn't come down here," he said. "It's up in the city. In the loops. In the 0's."

Her reply was dry and flat. "If he does come into the lower tunnels the barricades might discourage him."

Tempted to tell her how fast the Fluger could bore through her concrete walls, Addard held his tongue. Then he wished he had gone ahead and said it. Her spies must have seen to it that she was well informed.

"I'm aware that he can get through them if he wants to but he doesn't know about any city other than Olympus, and I hope to keep him in ignorance if I can," she said.

66

"By cutting off all dealings with us?"

"Why sound so indignant? We both know you'd do the same thing. My only regret is that now I won't be receiving any more news from you. Will I?"

"That's right," he said. "I'll see to it that every bit of intercommunication ceases. I don't have to worry about the Fluger destroying Olympus. You're going to do it. This was your idea, I take it? You've convinced the other cities that they should shut themselves away from me?"

"Of course. However, the only destruction you need fear is from the alien. Excuse me, I should say aliens. After you get rid of them the rest of us will lend you whatever you require to get back on your feet."

He wouldn't believe it, stood staring at the disconnected com as if it were his deadly enemy. In a reverse kind of logic, it was. The day of self-sustaining islands had passed and Wendelar was well aware of it. Olympus couldn't survive alone economically or any other way for very long. The boycott wouldn't hurt Superior. Wendelar had all the other cities.

As he traveled back the other way in the cab he gave the concrete wall a last look. He felt small and spiteful. How lovely it would be to capture the Fluger, bring him down here and sic him onto the blonde traitor.

Quantro Tilzer was jailed for suspicion of dope dealing.

"You're mistaken," he said. "What type of dope?"

"Astral," said the arresting officer.

"Now I know you're mistaken. Astral dope? What's that? What kind of dope is it?"

"The kind that makes folks think they're leaving their bodies and projecting into thin air, only all they're doing is flopping in some gutter or jumping off a balcony like that young fellow last week. Married less than a month and he takes a long, long dive after visiting your salon."

The words made Quantro wince. "I dislike hearing of the death of a youth, but you can't prove anything about dope and me."

It happened to be the truth, though the officer neglected to mention it. He personally had gone to Quantro's shop, paid his money and had some tea but the closest he came to astroing or projecting was when he fell up the steps after getting out of the cab that took him home. There had been dope in that tea, he knew. It tasted funny.

"The eye exercises and rituals are a bunch of baloney, so why don't you admit it?" he said. He wasn't particularly large or muscular but he felt as if he were physically capable of breaking the suspect in half at the moment.

"Exercises? Rituals?"

"If you didn't drink so much you'd recognize me even if I did wear a disguise into your place."

The barber peered with interest at the thin, young face and finally smiled. "But you didn't follow my instructions, did you? Oh, well, forget I said that. I'm a little tipsy now but it's only because of that monster living on the junk pile behind my apartment. You'd drink too if you had that to contend with."

"What's the stuff you're using? According to our records you're a graduate chemist so we figure you're making it yourself. Eliminates the risk of buying it from a source."

"Your imagination has gone berserk. I'm a bachelor barber who has his friends in now and then for a drink."

"Of tea?"

"Of plain water if that's what they want."

"The records we have on you say you're a genius. I say so what? You're killing people, mister, and you're going to fall to the tune of twenty years outside."

"I've killed no one. Can I help it if people are fools?"

"What's that supposed to mean?" The officer sounded hopeful. Perhaps a confession was in the offing.

"It simply means people are fools, including you. I get up in the morning and go to my place of business, I cut hair all day and I go home. Six days a week. I have a few friends, I like Scotch—"

"Or rye, or rotgut or anything else you can suck."

"It's a free city." Quantro stroked his white beard and belched. "You must make me comfortable all the while I'm a prisoner. It's the law and I demand my rights. I'm thirsty."

"How about some tea?"

"I implore you not to keep me here tonight. It's important that I be in the alley behind my apartment at least once every evening."

"Why? Do you have dope there?"

68

"No. The monster on the trash pile. If you salaried people did your jobs there wouldn't be any trash anywhere. He might tear up my apartment if I'm not present to blow my perfume around." Quantro shivered. "He might even be in my living room waiting for me."

"Let's get some vital statistics recorded before I lock you up. You're drunk, but not incurably so. Take my advice and don't try to plead insanity at the trial. We throw nuts out the door every day, believe me. Let's see, you're a white, adult male of more or less normal development. Name, we got that. Address, we got that. Height, a hundred and seventy-three centimeters, weight, eighty-one kilos, character all bad. Hmmm. You had some correspondence courses in miniature electronics. Quite a few courses. What did you do that for?"

"A hobby," Quantro said. "Woe is me if I don't get home before dark. That thing's waiting for me to come in smelling clean, and you took my flask, which I expect you to give back to me as soon as I step out of the joint. That'll be five minutes after my lawyer gets here."

The officer didn't respond but kept touching keys on the recorder. In a few moments he would have a complete tape and film on the prisoner.

"Why don't you turn me loose? You have nothing on me. I know you don't like me but is that any reason to get me killed? That monster in my back yard isn't anything to fool with. Big as a nightmare. Caught a glimpse of him once. Yellow. Ugly. Like the *tev* says, you know."

"Tev?"

"What's the matter with you? Can you speak in nothing but monosyllables? I'm talking about the UKO. The thing that's doing all the killing. It's yellow and larger than a rhinoceros. It lives in a junk pile behind my apartment, and the only reason it hasn't killed me is that it doesn't like the smell of booze."

The officer promptly forgot all about dope and astral projection. He was cousin to one of the mayor's advisers. Ennesto would want to hear about this.

* * *

Corradado burrowed deep into the junk pile to get away from the stink in the air. He could have found another dark retreat but didn't because one day soon he intended to kill the smelly little squeaker who came into the alley night after night. Besides, the pile reminded him of home for some reason, not that he was suffering from any homesickness but he didn't mind an infrequent recollection of moments or experiences on Fluga.

He was waiting for the squeaker to come down the alley and toss a crate or bottle onto the pile. Now that he thought about it, he had been waiting quite a while. The squeaker was late. Very late.

Something stirred in the big creature's brain, perhaps a little bell-like toll of warning, or perhaps he was disgruntled because he disliked having his expectations come to naught. At any rate he burrowed deeper into the pile, not recklessly as he usually moved, but cautiously and gently. In fact, he had nearly reached the bottom of the high mound when the sky seemed to fall and hit him in the back.

In actuality it was several tons of sand and large rocks dropped from a height of about thirty meters straight down through the section's ceiling by a crew of men acting on orders from Ennesto.

A point of trivia was the fact that had the load been dropped squarely on the alien's broad dome he would merely have sunk down into the garbage and on into the flooring to a depth of a few meters while the energy of the blow was absorbed by his incredibly impervious, heavy mass.

He was already at floor height, or depth, and he simply bent and snarled as he waited for the load to settle above him. His first impulse was to come up out of the debris and leap toward the ceiling, for he knew the attack had come from that direction. Then he calmed and remained still. The ceiling was too high and he would only waste strength trying to reach the squeakers who had done this. However, if he lay low and pretended they had injured or killed him. . . .

It was a long time before he heard them coming. They were hesitant, even reluctant to step into the alley. The purr of the digging machine they had brought with them was scarcely louder than their footfalls. Step by cautious step they walked, carrying their lights, murmuring in low tones, while the thing they feared hunched in the trash and worried that they might change their minds and go away. Of course, they were already too near to escape him, but he anticipated seeing their faces when he shot out into the open like a fanged juggernaut.

What they looked like were petrified corpses. There were six of them, four whites and two blacks but they were all more ashen in color than anything else, standing like little sticks of chalk and not even squealing, so great was their astonishment and foresight.

One by one their heads were bitten off and buried in the pile, far apart and at different depths so that those who came later wouldn't have an easy time gathering the body parts for burial. The visitor from space was learning more every day about the opposition.

After mangling the tractor, he went on a rampage along the entire block, tearing straight through the side of Quantro's apartment, pausing a few moments to make certain he wasn't there and then continuing into the next apartment and then the next until he emerged into a boulevard half a kilometer away. None of the buildings had been occupied.

Had Ennesto spent more thought than emotion regarding his strategy he might have considered the protest rally in progress some two kilometers west in an open boulevard. People didn't like the fact that they were confined to Olympus and couldn't travel to any of the other cities, so they had gathered to complain about it. Ennesto would also have considered the known information concerning the Fluger. He had read dozens of facts but had either forgotten or didn't think it significant that the alien's sense of hearing was quite keen.

Corradado was angry because Quantro hadn't been at home. When he heard squeaking sounds coming from the air-conditioning units in the walls of all the boulevards and rooms he traversed, he followed them.

Those spectators near the junk pile who had not been involved in the slaughter hung back and reported on the Fluger's movements. They knew which way he was headed, but by then it was too late to squelch the rally and clear the boulevard. Public speakers were trying to broadcast above the noise of the crowd, telling everyone that the UKO might possibly but not definitely enter their midst. At first only a few received the message; then gradually the news circulated so that by the time Corradado sprang through the western archway everyone was on the move. There was much squeaking and squealing.

Not having ascertained the exact direction in which the UKO was supposed to be traveling, some of the two or three hundred ran toward the wrong exit. Like a starving lion in an arena of old, the Fluger climbed all over the runners, bit them, clawed them, chewed, swiped, each of his attacking motions fatal to someone. Men and women fell one after another before an assault that became even more savage, while the street grew slippery and the squeals changed to moans.

There were police officers on the scene with their ineffectual weapons and there were heroes and martyrs, but Corradado took note of nothing but the count. He was delirious with numbers. How many could he kill before the boulevard was empty of life? How many would escape? How many corpses would there be and how high could he stack them?

Hulian was picked up by a pair of conscientious citizens and taken to the office of a man named Garly, who asked him how long he had been in the city.

"A couple of weeks." Hulian looked into the cold face of the mayor's adviser and decided he liked him, but only because the Fluger needed to be run down. In any peaceful situation he would have avoided Garly like a disease.

"You're lucky," said the adviser. "That is, if you don't become a fatal statistic. It doesn't matter whether I return you to your slum or ignore you. The law these days is somewhat irrelevant. Beat it." To the two citizens he said, "Get back to your jobs. They're more important than a hundred adolescent wetbacks."

Outside and free, Hulian walked toward an archway leading to a cab station. Curious to see what was more important than a hundred dirty people like himself, he followed the two citizens, squeezed into the same cab with them and took a long ride down the western support pillar of the city. Toward the end of the journey, when they switched to a final cab, he didn't get in with them but caught the very next one that came along. The two had been threatening to make a detour and take him someplace where he would be held in detention. It was dangerous down here, they said, no place for a kid; he belonged in the last three eastern sections with all the other children. Or, they said, probably hoping to turn him away or perhaps just being nasty, maybe he belonged in a clinic for deformed people. Wasn't he a freak? What had those slum parents of his been like to have given him one dark brown eye and a bright blue one?

Their destination was a lower cab tunnel where a frozen meat supply heading for Superior had been held up by the concrete barrier across the track. For three days. Backed up behind those hundred cabs were another hundred laden with fresh produce, and behind them was a week's sludge that was supposed to have been hauled outside and dumped in the wilderness of Tennessee. For three days the Fluger had been on a rampage just a few tunnels northward, and orders had come down for all activity to cease. The workers were to avoid drawing attention to themselves. No one wanted the UKO in any section of Olympus, but he surely wasn't wanted amid cabs of rotting meat and sludge. In the meantime the police were doing what they could to keep him busy.

In the tunnel, workers stayed by the barricade and waited for an all-clear signal so that they could renew their assault with drills and tractors. Soundings indicated the concrete was six meters thick, but it was newly poured and there was a chance they could get through. After the Fluger moved elsewhere they could even try breaking through the areas between tunnels. Meanwhile, they sat with the stalled cabs and tried to keep them from leaking.

The smell soon drove Hulian away. Appreciating his newfound freedom, he wandered through abandoned tunnels, ransacked storage rooms, rode cabs and all the time searched for a weapon. Though he already knew that guns, knives and bludgeons were no good, still he yearned for the feel of his old sword.

Eventually he came to a relatively safe level where there were empty walkways and unoccupied boulevards. Not that it offered them genuine security, but people were staying inside

73

with their exterior archways sealed by panels, their *tevs* tuned to news stations and their ears alert for the sounds of mindless rending. They had all heard and seen the UKO by now, either with their own eyes or on the *tev* screen. Hideous he was, and disastrous, like the plagues promised in *Revelations*. Never mind the story that he was supposed 'to be an odd but benevolent subject. He was from another planet, as were those other two aliens, the winged man and the furry scourge, and they were all dangerous. No matter how the government kept trying to protect them by keeping them in ignorance, people guessed more and more of the truth.

Alone, Hulian entered a kitchen on a boulevard, used some coins Roxey had given him and purchased a lunch of hamburger and creamed cauliflower. Sitting at a table, he looked through the archway and watched the *tev* suspended over the center of the street. The news kept changing hourly. Now the police were ordered to shoot the winged man and the black animal. Olympus had three deadly enemies. Panic reigned.

Even more earnestly, Hulian wished for a weapon with which to kill the Fluger. Once the yellow alien was dispatched people might settle down and let the winged man and his four-legged friend alone. The two were friends, weren't they? Was that how one described such a relationship? The boy ate and pondered the situation.

As he sat there he became aware of a burning pain in his elbow. Looking around at it, he noticed a small bubble on the skin. Gazing up at the relatively low ceiling of the kitchen, he observed a thick mass of yellowish substance growing in one spot, bulging and letting loose tiny droplets. Shortly the entire quantity would fall straight down onto the place where he sat.

Leaping from his seat, he was just in time to avoid a sudden pouring of yellow matter that hit the back of the chair and left a seeping, smoking trail in the metal. The cushion began to disintegrate, allowing the stuff to fall onto the floor where it began eating its way through.

The source of the acid was the ceiling of the boulevard directly above the kitchen. Hulian carefully searched for and found an el exiting into the boulevard a level higher. As soon as he walked through the archway he saw the man who was

74

responsible, white-haired but not really old, mad of expression and full of intent, standing on top of a street cleaner, shooting gas-powered arrows into a pipe that ran from ceiling to floor. The effluence from the pipe burned through the tile and leaked into the lower boulevards.

"Hey!" Hulian yelled, ready to jump. The man turned and fired at him. The missile traveled at almost blinding speed, burying into the wall beside his head. "Hey!" Hulian yelled again.

"I didn't kill anyone!" Quantro Tilzer shouted as he tried his best to pin down the bobbing target. "They're liars! That fellow went home to his wife just like he said he would. He didn't jump off any balcony!"

A lightbulb went on in Hulian's head and he immediately knew what this was about. He had seen cases of heavy conscience before. "Yes, he did!" he yelled. "I was there! He thought he was projecting, that he could fly like a bird. I tried to stop him, but he kicked my hands away and went over!"

These days Quantro went from one emotional extreme to another, staying far too long in the valleys and nadirs between. "Liar!" he bellowed, and fitted another arrow into his bow. Flame flared as it shot into the air but his aim was worse than usual and it went awry.

Hulian stepped back through the exit, traveled to the next highest boulevard, located an intercom and pushed one of the buttons.

"Welfare here. What is it?" The man on the screen waited patiently.

Hulian pushed another button.

"Code, please," said the operator, whose face didn't appear. "Domestic code, please."

He tried the bottom button on the panel.

"Security, yes?" said the woman on the screen.

"I want to report a crazy man. Section Four, Boulevard Seventeen. He's shooting arrows into a pipe and it's leaking acid everywhere. He shoots at people, too." After turning off that code, he punched another button and kept punching buttons until someone answered whom he wanted.

"Police department."

"I want you to leave my friend alone. He isn't like us, maybe, but he isn't a threat to anybody except the Fluger. Just because he can fly and run like a leopard is no reason for you to try to kill him."

"Which friend is that, son?" said the man on the screen. Someone behind him spoke and he turned for a brief moment. Again looking at Hulian, he said, "What's your friend's name?"

"I don't know. He never told me, but he's kind and you're stupid for going after him. Why don't you leave him alone and kill the Fluger?"

"Do you know where he lives or where he's staying?"

"No."

"What about his contacts? I mean besides yourself?"

"What does that mean?" said Hulian.

The man smiled. "I'd simply like to know if he's gregarious like human beings. He must go places, eat, talk to others, do things people do."

"Of course he does all that. He isn't some kind of monster." It suddenly dawned on Hulian that the other's smile wasn't a friendly one but in fact was little more than a chill grimace. He wasn't making common conversation. Why did he stay there on the screen? Why not say good-bye and turn off?

The boy turned and walked away from the intercom, practically into the arms of two men who stepped from a down el. Two other men emerged from an up el at nearly the same moment. He hadn't known it required mere seconds to locate an activated intercom and no more than another ten or fifteen seconds for a roving patrol to arrive.

Chapter VIII

Desiring even the poor security of a jail, Quantro stood on the street cleaner and waited for them to come and take him away. Indeed, they would have if someone hadn't gotten to him first.

The initial patrol picked up Hulian and hurried him to a cab station while a second group rode an el down a column in the center of the boulevard near the kitchen. Meanwhile, a man with wings swooped down from a decorative opening in the eastern archway near the ceiling; snatched up the archer and flew back up to the opening. It was large enough for him to step through. From there he flew unseen along the ceilings of several boulevards until he reached an opening leading to the outside. He took his captive up over the city and came to rest squarely on top of the fifth loop or 0.

Like most Olympians, Quantro occasionally experienced moments of claustrophobia, but generally he preferred the closed walls of home. Now he found himself in the widest of open spaces in the hands of a creature who was in no way human. Or hardly in any way.

The top of the 0 was so large that he did not suffer from vertigo, but the huge sky and sun made him feel as if he were an insect about to be crushed.

"How do you like it?" said Kam Shar.

Instead of running or crawling away, Quantro hugged the surface under him and groaned, "I don't! Take me down!"

"I've observed that open space usually terrifies Kappans

who live within high cities. I want you to remember your fear, because if you don't cooperate with me I'm going to bring you back up here and abandon you."

"No, no, I'll cooperate, only get me down. No, not that way! I don't want to fly anymore!"

They were airborne as quickly as it took the alien to lift him and flap his strong wings. His mouth full of wind, Quantro screamed a silent scream. He found himself grasping the detestable creature more tightly than he would have a friend, but only until they landed and he assured himself that the ground under his feet was solid. Then he broke away and began to run. All by himself. Toward nowhere. There was nothing but kilometers of grass in every direction, and sky overwhelming him, with a yellow sun that threatened to hit him on the head. Besides which he wasn't well. He began screaming again and this time he didn't stop until he fell over in an exhausted faint.

He had seen slum houses and slum towns on film, so when he came to his senses he knew where he was, not exactly which slum town, of course, but at least he was aware of where the alien had parked him. The place reminded him of the junk pile behind his old apartment but smelled much worse.

His kidnapper sat on a wrecked couch watching him. He lay on a dusty floor among children's broken toys, dirty dishes, something that looked like an inner tube, pots and pans and various other debris.

"What planet are you from?" he said, sitting up. He disguised his feelings, made his voice amiable. He couldn't tell then, just as he could never tell whether or not he deceived the other.

"Eldoron. My name is Kam Shar."

"What'd you bring me out here for?"

"To show you where you'll live for the rest of your life if you don't do what I tell you."

Feeling a new wave of panic washing over him, Quantro made himself sit quietly. "All I have to do is go to any entrance into Olympus and let them have my fingerprints, or just a hair on my head or one from my beard and they'll let me right in."

"Not if I removed your identity from the computer files."

"I've lived a long time. Records on me are all over the place."

78

"You know they always refer to the main computer in most matters."

Quantro's voice betrayed his emotions. "Why would you do it? Why pick on me?"

"I was hired to kill the UKO. The Fluger. You're going to help me."

Once again Quantro fainted. For the second time in his life the world became an enclosure of buzzing black specks, and he fell over into the junk left behind by the shack's former tenants, who had either been killed or frightened away by the yellow murderer. Awakening at dusk he had the weird and unbelievable experience of seeing how a wood fire in an open grate could hold back the darkness.

There was no use trying to have an ordinary conversation with his kidnapper. The man simply wasn't human, didn't think like a human, wasn't interested in small talk or any kind of talk that wasn't related to his mission.

He was offered food from cans on wall shelves; disdainfully refused it. Everybody knew slum people ate garbage, the stuff Olympians fed their hogs. That it came from cans appearing clean and sterile made no difference.

"I was a chemist for a long time," he said, exasperated by the interminable questioning. There were too many queries and besides, he was exhausted. Also his nerves were frayed. He couldn't envision his exit scene from this environment and that made him anxious.

"The electronic tapes?" he said. "Listen, I don't know where you got your information but it's all wrong. There really is such a thing as astral projection."

Kam Shar sat before the fire and warmed his hands. "I told you I would leave you here permanently. Stop lying. You fed your customers dope. When they did the eye exercises or when they recited the chants or performed the rituals they set off the electronic signal on the tape wrapped around the hallucinogen. What I'm asking you now is, what was the code? The signal? What started the reaction?"

"How do you know all this? How did you find out? Who told you?"

"No one. I've seen it all before."

79

"Where?" said Quantro. "Which section? Who's trying to take over my operation?"

"That isn't even mildly humorous. I mean I've seen things on other worlds."

Quantro looked at the wings jutting up out of the blouse. They grew like extensions of the shoulder blades, big and long and folded, making Kam Shar look like a tall, skinny bird. They were black and shiny in the flickering light from the fire. The alien sat hunched toward the heat.

"It's warm where you come from, isn't it? You don't like the cold."

"Yes, it's warm. No, I don't like the cold. Tell me about the code. Is it a word?"

Quantro gave up. It didn't matter anyway. This wasn't a man, only a freak from the stars. "Part of one," he said. "It's a syllable."

Kam Shar shook his head. "That would make it too risky. Can you base it on anything else?"

"Like what?"

"Can you?"

"I don't know. What have you been thinking? Don't tell me you're planning to feed that yellow beast some of my astral dope?"

"No, that isn't my plan. What I have in mind for him won't send him into ecstasies or flights of fancy."

Maybe this was the time for wheedling. It wouldn't hurt to try. "You don't need me," said Quantro. "I can tell by talking to you that you're very bright, too much so to be needing the likes of an Earthman who hadn't done much good in his life. Why don't you just point me the way to Olympus and I'll leave you here with your important thoughts?"

"No."

"I'm a drinker. An alcoholic. I'll only get in your way."

"You won't."

"You don't know what we're like. We hate foreigners. We hate anybody we don't understand. Anyone who isn't like us is an object of scorn and ridicule."

"I'm uninterested in your personal opinions."

"There's one you'd better be interested in. I can't work when I'm sober. My brain is pickled."

80

'What do you mean?"

'I mean I can only do my thing when I'm sopping wet."

"I don't understand."

"I need a bottle!" roared Quantro.

Hulian wasn't frightened. Not much. He had been in this office before, when Kam Shar the flier brought him here and left him with Kam Shar the man. The alien wasn't present now, which was unfortunate since he was a friend, while the four men standing around his chair asking him questions were definitely not friendly and were very probably his enemies.

"He gave you that blue eye?" Ennesto said again. "How did he do it? Did he carry his own medical kit?"

"No, he did it in one of your clinics."

"Which one?" .

"I don't know. I was unconscious most of the time."

"He doesn't have much sense, does he? Anybody with eyes can see it wasn't the right color. Now hear me, lad. You cooperate with us and I'll personally see that you get another blue eye the same color as that one. It'll make you mighty handsome."

Hulian stared up at the lined old face in wonder. What made Ennesto think he didn't want to exchange the blue eye for another brown one like his own? He kept staring until he realized the old man's eyes were blue. Sort of. They were watery and pale but they were blue.

Garly said, "We're wasting time. Give him a hypo and he'll be happy to tell us where Kam Shar hid his extra bodies."

"It's against the law," said Addard.

"Dear me," said Ennesto.

"That was always an asinine law," said Garly. "Why have truth serum if you need a subject's permission to use it on him?"

"Forget it," said Addard. "I won't do it. He's only a child. He'll tell us." To Hulian he said, "You want to be a citizen of Olympus, I know. Fine, we'll make you a citizen."

"Olympus is being destroyed by the Fluger," said Hulian. "You'll all be living in slum towns before this is over."

Ennesto hit him. Before Addard could protest he said "Every time he says something like that I'm going to bash him. You know how old I am? Ninety-two. Never will I live in a slum town, and he'd better not even hint that I will." Glaring down at Hulian, he said, "Just answer the questions and don't be wise."

"It didn't hurt." Hulian blinked back the tears threatening to spill over. His head felt as if the old man had hit him with a tree.

"We aren't going to hurt you," said Monkwell. Speaking to the others he said, "Are we? Was that the last blow to be struck in this illustrious gathering? It had better have been."

"Take a walk," said Garly. "Only be sure the Fluger isn't anywhere nearby."

They kept talking and Hulian sat and tried to figure it out in his mind. They had hired Kam Shar to kill the Fluger, and he was trying to do his job, so why were they trying to kill him? Why did they want to know where his bodies were hidden?

He asked them and they said Kam Shar was out of control. The alien must be kept under control. Why? When he asked that, they looked at him as if he were too dense ever to understand. Why did they need to know where the two extra bodies were? To give them control. Would he never comprehend anything? Control was something they had to have.

"I don't see why," he said. "Why don't you leave them alone? Is it because he makes you feel unimportant?"

Ennesto hit him again.

"I'm leaving," said Monkwell. "I might not be the brightest person in this group but I know what I can and can't stomach. You're beating on this kid to get rid of your own stupid frustrations." No one said anything and he left.

The city had always functioned as a comfortable home for its human occupants because it was pampered and cared for like the infants in Section Eight. No one but the insane had ever deliberately damaged any part of it; like Earth, it was a solitary oasis in a desert of emptiness. Without the city there were only wilderness, slums and dependence upon the land, and who knew anything about that or even wanted to know? Olympus was the beloved country. It was home. The machines constituting her heart were daily maintained. More man-hours were spent seeing to working parts than to any other task.

It was different now. There weren't enough hours in the day to repair the damage done by the yellow invader. No single crew with its complement of tractors and hand tools could repair a ruined cab tunnel and make it operational again before the Fluger destroyed another. One by one the tunnels were closing. People had to walk wherever they went, which meant they didn't go far. No crew could quickly clean up the destruction caused by leaking acid, gas or oil, so more rooms, boulevards and sections were closing to the public. It was common knowledge that the Fluger had staked out one of the reservoirs as his private drinking fountain. The remaining reservoirs, the smaller ones, the more isolated ones deep in the western column, had to be drawn upon for the city's supply because no one dared go near the other to check its maintenance levels.

Farming was a pursuit that went on all the time; trade with the other cities had been profitable, but now the produce stagnated in cabs in the lower tunnels. It also lay rotting on the ground under the crooked light pouring night and day from grilled ceilings. Some of the farmers had taken to carting the excess into empty corridors and leaving it there. Had the windows opened onto the outside, they would have thrown it out. That would have been one solution to the problem, but the windows weren't real and didn't open onto anything but other corridors clogged with trash, broken furniture and machines in need of repair.

Disliking the outside, Olympians were fast realizing how much their survival depended upon it. If access to it didn't soon become a great deal easier they would smother in their own garbage.

Roxey was on call in Section Four, gymnasium number thirty-six. He was trying to get into gymnasium number fifty-two but had finally abandoned all attempts to do it the normal way.

"I'm going to climb up the wall shaft and break in," he told his chief crewman, who knew better than to argue. Roxey usually made up his mind in a hurry. Once that was done it was done. Not even the men from Security had anything to say about it. They carried paralysis guns and seemed to want things to go their way. However, they must have had orders to defer to the big, blind foreman because they did as they were told.

The weight of debris on the next level had broken the ceiling, and chunks of concrete blocked the western entrance into number fifty-two gymnasium. A fire had burned away the floor by the eastern entrance. His radar unit working at top performance, Roxey waited for his men to cut a hole in the wall near the western archway, shouldered his way in and started climbing.

The inner walls of the shaft were corrugated with horizontal beams, the space between slightly more than one meter, so it wasn't difficult for him to step onto a beam on one side, holding onto both sides with his hands, and then step onto the next highest beam.

He knew exactly where everything was, could locate the tiny cobwebs missed by the big vacuum cleaners that covered nearly every hidden and unhidden centimeter of Olympus. The very dust in the air failed to go unnoticed by him but betrayed its presence by sending little pinging sounds back through his hearing instrument. He knew everything but color. How thick was the beam upon which he was about to step? Not only could he answer with surety but he could also state the beam section's approximate weight, density, smoothness and strength. Were it fibers compact or loose? Was the wood splintering on the surface? What about the beam overhead that he was about to grasp? Roxey knew all the answers.

With the drill kit strapped to his back he cut a sizable hole in the wall near the floor of gymnasium fifty-two and stepped through. After the others followed him in they shot hooks into the decorative openings near the ceiling, hoisted themselves up and checked all the vent openings, air shafts and niches. The only thing in them was dust. There were no bodies, unconscious, dead, alive or otherwise.

The men from Security seemed disappointed and insisted upon having a second look at everything. They were finally convinced that they would find nothing and went their own way, back down the wall shaft.

Leaving his crew to build a new threshold at the eastern archway, Roxey followed the guards, located an intercom and called Ennesto.

"Cleared out, did he?"

"Looks like it," said Roxey.

"He has all of Olympus to find another hiding place."

Roxey was thinking it was a waste of time to do anything but try to kill the Fluger but he didn't say it. It was more important than building new floors, opening cab tunnels or hunting for alien bodies. The city had become a series of dominoes that were toppling one after another. If something didn't happen to stop the natural sequence of events . . .

He was about to make some kind of response when a *tev* overhead flicked on. The announcer didn't sound excited but he looked terrified.

"The Fluger is in Section Seven, Level Six, headed east. The Fluger is in Section Seven, Level Six, headed east. The Fluger is in . . ." He said it over and over again, not pausing, emphasizing no word of it.

Roxey dropped the intercom and walked toward the nearest cab station. If the cabs didn't work he would take to the inner els, and if they were blocked he would ride exterior els and climb through the openings at the ceilings. He would scale bare walls if he had to but he was going to get to Section Seven, Level Six, Boulevard Nineteen before the Fluger. On the other side of that boulevard was the beginning of Section Eight where the children lived. All the young. The life of Olympus, the reason why everyone worked, built, ate, lived. The kids. The Fluger was headed their way.

Boulevard Number Nineteen was one of the largest in the city, made that way as a special marker because it divided the city and its future. Children, some parents, teachers, nannies, social workers, juvenile courts, schools, practically everything that had to do with the nurturing of the young were situated in Sections Eight to Ten. There were many levels in the sections. There were many children.

Corradado prowled at his leisure along the causeway of Level Six. In no hurry, he paused to knock down a statue that was in his way. He had broken many such impediments, hating their smoothness, the shine of their surface, the look of care about them, the earnest shrieker expressions on the fronts of the heads. Some had their hands extended, or a foot thrust forward, or some held objects or sat on animals or in machines. It didn't matter to the Fluger. He smashed them one and all whenever and wherever he saw them.

At times he paused to sharpen his claws on something. The something had to be hard and rough and there weren't too many appropriate objects in Olympian corridors, so whenever he felt like it he ripped a hole in a wall or floor and used a jagged edge of concrete. It was unsatisfactory, though, the concrete crumbling as soon as he applied the least pressure.

By the time he approached Boulevard Nineteen, he was bored and cross. His toes itched, his ears throbbed, his throat felt raw, in general he didn't feel well. Perhaps the shriekers hoped he had fallen dead from one of their diseases, but his body was merely preparing itself for its annual sleep. One of these days he would find a dark and comfortable place, perhaps inside a rock, and sleep for a week. But not now. Not today. This was the time when he drew near Boulevard Nineteen and his interest was piqued because of the silence coming from it. No matter where he went in Olympus shriekers made their sounds and fled before him. Always. Now they were behaving differently. They weren't running and they were silent.

He disdained entering through the archway but swiped a section out of the wall with a practiced swing of a paw and barreled on through.

Chapter IX

Roxey didn't feel like a martyr. He didn't feel heroic or brave. What he felt at this point was that he was expendable. If civilization and survival were on the line, and it seemed to be where the young were concerned, then he had to go and add his body to the multitude crammed onto the boulevard.

Even after Corradado made his appearance, people kept adding their flesh and bones to the crowd, entering from cab stations and els, riding down walls in the open cars, squeezing in through the eastern archway. Some even crawled through the openings near the ceiling and climbed down ropes.

There were no weapons. They hadn't had time to arm themselves and besides there was scarcely space for their bodies on the packed causeway. The fact was that if the Fluger wanted into Section Seven he would have to cross over and through thousands of human beings.

It would have been a simple matter for him to bore through the masses to the archway leading to the next section, but his emotional makeup was such that after having vented his rage upon an enemy, he grew to hate that enemy even more. He had hated the shriekers from the moment he killed and consumed his first victim and his ire daily increased until the very thought of them incensed him to great fury.

They were everywhere. There wasn't any place that they couldn't be seen and felt. They were in front of him, beneath, on top, striking at him, gouging his face, attacking his hindquarters. It never dawned on him that they might be trying to kill him, and it probably never entered the minds of those in the crowd that there was a remote chance of crippling him. They were simply presenting him with what they hoped was an insurmountable obstacle, and if it wasn't good enough their lives like their deaths would have been and would be meaningless.

He managed to get approximately a third of the way across the boulevard before his right eye puffed and leaked fluid. For the first time in a very long time the big yellow creature experienced frustration. It didn't do him any good to knock a whole bunch of the shriekers out of the way, for when he did another took its place, a screaming, squealing horde of the enemy who died with rage on their faces, who used their fists to beat at him, their fingers to grab at him, their fingernails to rip at his parts.

One man went so far as to grip his right eye with two hands and try to yank it out, even while he was being cut in half by grinding teeth. The Fluger was blinded by the blood on his head, not his own, but it didn't matter since he still couldn't see. The sheer weight of the mob turned him onto his back and the shriekers tore at his belly and private parts. They did him no lasting damage, but it would be many a day before he hadn't some ache or pain to remind him of how the puny little people had ganged up on him.

Startled by the resistance, he entertained no thoughts as to why they had chosen this particular place to make their stand. While he sprawled on his back and rent human flesh with his claws, someone took a long object and tried to pierce his throat. The point of the thing was sharp enough to bite in but there was no blood, no oozing of vital matter, because the Fluger's outer skin was smooth and impenetrable, like molten metal, like shifting sand, like the cloaks of hell to the would-be assassin, who had taken a thin, half-meter-long spike to the yellow neck. Corradado looked at the man with savage eyes, bit him in two and spat the parts onto the others clambering onto him.

Somehow the idea infiltrated the minds of those closest to the alien that though they couldn't hurt him, they might be able to move him. People blocking the western entrance climbed across their brethren, while those beside the Fluger shoved him. By the dozens they died and more walked over the corpses to take their places. Little by little the plan became apparent to all, and people were quicker to move out of the way, to pull bodies aside, to get behind the shovers and add their weight and strength.

Kicking and clawing, mewling, roaring, coughing, trying to kill enough so that he could get onto his feet, Corradado was taken to the archway and carried through it. He was incredulous. Like a mountain of bread being borne off by an army of ants, he found himself moving across a causeway toward a large balcony. The roar of the shriekers was deafening and he marveled even more at their insanity until he saw the sky beyond the balcony and realized they intended to throw him off.

It might have been a technical point as to whether or not a fall off Mount Olympus would kill him, but he wasn't interested in finding out. At first he had gone along for the ride, having grown weary from so much activity, but now he let out a tremendous roar, steeled his mighty muscles, used the bodies under him as a brace and sprang straight up into the air.

He might have come down upon his tormentors, could easily have slaughtered them and then gone back into the boulevard and freed Earth of every living soul there. His once shiny coat was matted and filthy, his claws were filled with the debris of stinking meat, his mouth was bitter with the taste of hair and clothing. Also his right eye pained him. There was something else. For the first time he was experiencing fear.

Instead of taking revenge, he allowed his spring to carry him up to a solid wall beside the balcony. Rebounding at an angle, he landed on the floor well away from his attackers; before they could get him again he ran.

It had to be a first, the retreat of the alien. He didn't consider it as such, if indeed he considered it at all. His only desire was to be alone where he could see to his grooming, enjoy a little rest, indulge in some minor reflecting. Surely he was loose among strange maniacs.

One of the maniacs who pursued him through the next boulevard was Roxey. Not having gotten close enough to be hurt or killed by the alien, the big man nevertheless had been squeezed by the crowd so that as he ran with the others he gasped and fought to catch his breath. Having worked in the area before, he was familiar with its cab tunnels and storage sheds and guessed the Fluger might soon take to one of the lower levels to get away from his hunters.

He ran down a set of stairs to a cab station, stepped into the first vehicle that came along and rode it for the space of two boulevards. The Fluger might go on down to the next level and its sections, but there was the chance he might be satisfied to travel in this tunnel. The human had no plan to try to corner and attack the alien, but if he could find out where it intended to stop and rest he could alert Security.

He would have been better off had he run along the tunnel and not caught another cab. He had been on crews whose task it was to set up signals in damaged stations to warn citizens not to use the vehicles. Usually it was because the tracks were broken in places or the roof had fallen. He knew most people were walking these days, and the crews couldn't keep up with the necessity for placing warning signals in stations, not to mention repairing the tunnels.

His radar unit sometimes made him feel infallible. Into a cab he hurried, planning to traverse two more boulevards, below which the tunnels forked eight ways. If he were lucky the alien would choose one of those eight passages, and he would be there to see which it was. They all went on straight courses for many kilometers, which meant once the Fluger made his choice between them he would be committed long enough for Security to originate a plan. Unless, of course, the monster made his own tunnel in another direction, or turned back.

Roxey didn't find out which way the enemy went or if he even came down to that particular tunnel. The cab in which he rode was a sports model built to withstand the excessive vibration caused by high speed. When its passenger manipulated the controls rather than leave it on automatic, it shot down the pipe like a silver flash of light.

Unfortunately it didn't go far, not even halfway to the eight-fork junction, but instead suddenly dropped into empty space at an angle, so that instead of breaking up or exploding it was gradually slowed. There was a piercing shriek of metal on metal as the cab found a shaft into which to settle. Afterward it dropped straight down at a rapid pace for a good distance. It slowed as the shaft narrowed and closed in around it.

Roxey's unit had warned him of the hole where tracks had once been, and several moments before the cab pitched into it he managed to apply the brakes. Now he lay on the floor and waited for the fall into eternity. He knew the machine had hurtled into the space between two parts of a wall of a boulevard, just as he knew there was nothing between most of those parts but a crisscrossing of naked beams. If he slipped through there was nothing to stop him from plunging all the way to the ground.

The cab rocked and swayed when he moved, so he forced himself to lie still while his radar unit sounded out the situation. The only problem was that the unit couldn't penetrate the solid partitions of the cab, while the half door didn't allow for a great deal of probing.

Cautiously he inched his way to the opening, trying not to breathe, dry-mouthed and growing more so with every creak and groan made by his jostling world. His reality of darkness seemed blacker now that his life hung in the balance of the cab upon one or two beams of steel. No, they were wooden and there weren't two of them but only one. A corner of the cab rested on the junction of two wooden slats, while the machine itself was loosely wedged between the shaft walls. It fell as he climbed over the half door and grabbed another beam, dropped with a thud that threatened to shake him from his hold. He could hear it crashing and banging against the wall until finally it came to a stop a quarter kilometer below him.

Now there was no sound at all. Fragile though the partitions of the shaft had seemed when he was falling into it in the cab, they were thick enough to cut off all sounds of the city, so that he seemed to hang in an empty void. Not even the throb of the big engines running Olympus reached him here, and he straddled a wooden plank and felt the perspiration building on his back and thighs.

No sound. Nothing. His body felt as if it had turned to water. Being blind hadn't mattered so much to him for a long time but it mattered now. Somewhere during that climb, while he was hanging on and the cab was falling down into the shaft, he had lost his unit. Somehow the fastenings had failed and allowed it to drop out of his pocket. He wasn't as blind as a bat anymore. He was just blind.

He tried remembering how the place had looked while he climbed over the cab's half door. He hadn't been paying much attention. There was an aperture in the shaft wall, and he had gone through that onto the beam beyond, which was an extensive latticework of horizontal planks, like a web stretching for several meters ahead and to his right and left. How many meters? Could he estimate? Maybe eight, maybe ten. Maybe he hadn't really noticed, so intent was he upon getting out of the cab, through the hole and onto the plank. Now that he was here all he could do was clutch and perspire and try to hear pings that weren't there.

Angrily he grasped the plugs in his ears and threw them away, cried out as he swayed on his perch, finally lay on it while he tried to catch his breath. He couldn't stay there for more than a few minutes. The plank wasn't wide enough for him to relax. Where did a blind man go and what did he do when lost in the darkness without his ears?

He learned something as he scooted along the beam. The radar unit had been a lifesaver without a doubt, but he had placed too much reliance on it. Now he needed a good pair of ears; his own had lost most of their keenness. Over the years he grew so accustomed to the pinging sounds put out by the unit that he had lost his habit of turning it off at night or even lowering the volume: His own sounds were unfamiliar, strange, difficult to interpret.

From somewhere came a gust of air and he knew it was the vacuum cleaners reaching down into hidden depths to pick up dust and discourage insects and other vermin. Nothing lived down here very long. If the vacuums didn't suck it up, the disinfecting gas took care of it. Not that it was time for a gassing. This was Tuesday and they only did the shafts on Saturday. Fine. He had four days in which to crawl along narrow boards and try to find a way out.

It seemed to him that days passed before he found the four-legged, furry body that represented Kam Shar's number-three habitation. When he first touched it he thought it was the Fluger and prepared to throw himself into the darkness. However, the beast didn't move and in fact didn't even seem to be breathing. Also it was too small. It lay on a platform much more substantial than Roxey's plank. He tried to transfer to it but discovered the only way he could do it was to straddle the animal's back.

Exhausted, thirsty, convinced that he was soon to die, he gratefully sank into the soft fur and went to sleep. He was thankful that the creature failed to stir at his touch, was unaware of why it lay here in the darkness or how it had gotten here. He didn't care.

When life came into the beast he awakened at once. Crouching low on the furry back he buried his fingers in the thick hair, determined to hang on no matter how hard it bucked. Conceivably he wouldn't be killed if he were thrown off, since this area had to be between the floor of one level and the ceiling of another, yet he didn't know how far from each he was. Having crawled around for a considerable time stretching his arms and legs to feel for obstacles, he still hadn't determined the dimensions of the place.

"My name is Roxey," he said "Don't move, please, or I'll fall off. Listen to me."

He felt the animal relax.

"Have you seen Hulian?" he asked. "The boy? He hasn't

92

come home for several days. He was staying with me but he's disappeared."

Like a fur rug Kam Shar lay and seemed to doze.

"I don't know if you can understand me," said Roxey. "I was in a cab chasing the Fluger, and it fell into the shaft over there. I've been crawling around in here for at least three days."

Kam Shar stood up and waited while he caught his balance. "I don't know if I can hold on. I'm so tired."

Slowly the alien walked along a plank behind the platform. He continued for several minutes and finally stopped.

"What is it?" said Roxey. "What do you want me to do?" He reached out to see if anything was there. The other had probably come in there for privacy, and the only way was down, or up, which meant he had to climb or jump to another level, probably through a hole.

Having thought it would be impossible to get to a standing position, he stood on the broad back of Kam Shar's number-three form and reached up to grab a shelf-like protrusion. Since it wasn't too high, he managed to haul himself onto a platform and waited for the animal to come up beside him. It stayed where it was.

On his hands and knees he called down into the hole. "Hulian said you were his friend. He told me about you and I think I understand. I can't find him and I'm afraid he's in trouble."

He waited but there was no response and finally he stood and felt for another platform, climbed upon it and felt for the next. Eventually he crawled up into a cab station and out onto a boulevard.

In his day, Quantro Tilzer had been a fair chemist, that day being before he became addicted to alcohol. Now, when he saw what Kam Shar could do with elements, he surmised that he hadn't been abducted for any complicated task. In that he was correct. He was along to provide labels and define chemicals so that Kam Shar would know what he was working with.

The lab was in the slum town nearest the southwestern corner of Olympus, a clean brick building with white enameled furniture made of heavy aluminum. The cabinets were steel, also enameled white, the tables were high and sturdy, the vials, retorts and other equipment were crystal clear and sterile. Everything had been taken from Olympus and brought here.

If his companion hadn't persisted in switching his outward form, Quantro could have grown fond of the lab; there was always a full flask hidden somewhere in it, his property if he could find it. He seldom if ever failed to do that.

Now the experiment was drawing to its end. There weren't going to be any tests done, with the exception of the final one.

"You've ruined me for Olympus, you know?" he said to Kam Shar, who was just an ordinary man today, no wings, no black and heathenish hound's body. Just a man. Or nearly.

"How is that?"

Swaying as he usually did of late, Quantro said, "I used to think nothing could be done anywhere but in the city. Now I know anything can be done anywhere just so long as one has the tools and equipment."

"You'll have to cut down on your drinking, otherwise you won't be able to cut anyone's hair."

"It'll be no problem. I've cut down a thousand times. Do you think that hypo's painless?"

Kam Shar had one all prepared. "Yes, I think so. Let's make certain." Without warning he reached out and injected Quantro's forearm. "There. A person with a heavy conscience needs a challenge. I've just given one to you. It's for all those young people who flew from balconies and out of windows without wings. For all the others. You were in business a long time."

As he bent down to pick up a vial from the floor, Quantro hit him with the flask. Then the human ran, not looking back to check the results of his act, unconcerned that he might have split Kam Shar's skull but in fact wishing he had.

"What do you want from us?" said the slum chief. He stood at the foot of a grassy knoll accompanied by a dozen women, two dozen children and five young men. His name was Purly and he was old but he was enormous in size and plainly powerful.

94

Quantro had searched all through the town before he found them on the outskirts. "Asylum," he said. "A home."

One of the men snorted.

"Don't look to me like you can work," said Purly.

"Work? What do you want to work for? When you go to Olympus I'll go with you. Incognito. I'm not a citizen either."

"What you are is a liar." Purly's gray brows furrowed. "You think we don't know a citizen when we see one? I've been out here ten years, due to go back next week, so I know the difference between a soft-bellied Olympian and an outsider. Besides, we aren't going to the city."

"You just said you have but a week of your sentence left."

"True. Embezzlement. Ten years in hell. Now I think it may have been heaven. Or at least a better sanctuary than that rattrap Olympus where the rat has taken charge."

To Quantro's amazement the group turned as one and started up the hill. He couldn't believe it. Olympus and their wretched slum home were back the other way. "Wait!" he said. "Why can't I come with you?"

Purly waited for him to catch up. "You want to go to Olympus?"

"Yes, and I think you do, too. You're planning to circle the hill and head back."

"We're heading for some high caves. You're welcome to come along but you'll have to do your share of work."

"I don't want to go to any caves. What's the matter with you? Even the town back there is better than caves."

Purly looked irritated. "We know more about that Fluger than you do. He comes out here once in a while and knocks the devil out of everyone and everything. One thing he doesn't like too much is height. He won't go up the mountain."

"He's going to be killed."

"By the time you city slickers discover he isn't killable Olympus will be ruined. When he's had enough of it he'll come back outside to finish off all the survivors."

"And you and your group will be safe in the caves?"

"Right," said Purly.

"You're mad. If you go back to Olympus you'll be admitted right away and so will your wives and children."

Purly turned his back and walked away.

"All right. Let me come with you. I can't bear to be alone. I'll do my best to be useful."

"Maybe you can entertain us with tall stories," said the old man over his shoulder.

Quantro never reached the caves. At least he did get to see the mountain from a short distance, a bleak and lonely hump dotted with black holes.

He was lagging behind, perspiring, exhausted, ill with apprehension, desperately trying to think of some better future than being a cave dweller, when Purly came back to him.

"I think maybe you better forget about tagging along."

"What! You already said I could!"

Gesturing toward the sky, the other said, "I'm not going to argue with that."

It was Kam Shar, flitting back and forth high overhead.

"He's been with us ten minutes or so," said Purly. "I can tell you right off he doesn't want to join our group. Good thing, too, since he wouldn't be welcome. We've decided he's up there because he wants you."

"You don't understand."

"I don't want to, either. You just get."

"Wait, no, he's crazy! You can't turn me over to him. I'm a human being."

The big man shrugged. "Maybe you are and maybe you aren't. You haven't been around long enough for me to find out. Now listen to what I say. I don't want you taking another step up the mountain. You just wait here with that winged fellow."

"I don't want anything to do with him!"

"Nor do we. I'm going to join my people now, and we're going on up to the caves. Don't follow us or I'll shoot you in the leg." Purly took a pistol out of his knapsack. "In fact, I'll kill you deader than a rock if you don't do what I tell you."

Quantro watched him go. What a miserable group they were, ragged, thin, laden down with poor provisions, though at least in the caves they might have a chance. It was more than he had.

There was nothing for him to do but wait for Kam Shar to fly down and light beside him. Filled with horror, he could still view his predicament somewhat clinically, perhaps an aftereffect of all the whisky he had swilled that day. He would live as long as he didn't relinquish the desire to do so. Once he accepted his own extinction, he was a dead man. Such was the future or destiny the Eldoron gave him with the hypo.

After reading the note pinned to his front door, Roxey went to number one-fifty-nine clinic to pick up his son.

"Sir, according to our records, your son died eleven years ago in an accident. Along with his mother." The clerk was middle-aged, kindly and kept looking over his shoulder. Perhaps his dreams were cast with large yellow murderers.

"Your patient's name is Hulian," said Roxey. "I have Mr. Addard's permission to take care of him. He's thirteen, brown-skinned, one brown and one blue eye—"

"Oh, that one. I'm afraid he's comatose."

"How bad?"

"He has a fifty-fifty chance of going either way. Bed rest and feeding is all we can give him."

"I can give him that too."

Consulting the computer files, the clerk said, "He doesn't really belong to anyone. I can't just take your word. I'll have to check with someone higher up."

"Why don't you check with whoever brought him here?"

"We don't know who that was. He was left outside."

"You mean he was dumped?"

The clerk called his supervisor, who went even further up the line until finally an authority named Monkwell said to let the blind man have custody of the boy.

Back in his apartment, Roxey tended Hulian, laid cold compresses on his bruises, kept his throat and nostrils clear, diapered him twice a day, made certain the feeding lines were secure in his arms and waited for something to happen.

Addard sat staring at the tiny speck of blood on his forearm. "What have you done?" he said dazedly.

"It isn't because of the boy. It's because you're the leader. You must play a part in the reckoning. It's customary."

"I don't understand."

"You don't need to."

Daubing at the blood, Addard watched it disappear. He sat

at his office desk and felt like a reeling monarch, not because the Eldoron had hit him with a hypo but because it was simply a feeling engendered in him every time he went outside and saw something broken, bent, twisted, ruined. He stared at Kam Shar, who was standing, of course, and wondered why the alien's mild expression never changed.

"You've failed, too," he said. "We haven't been able to stop you, but neither have you done what you were paid for."

"The end has already begun."

"I'll try not to laugh at that remark. My world is going to break my head when it topples."

"I would have accomplished more by now if you hadn't sent your men to hunt my bodies."

"You mean your burial places. Like Dracula. Why don't you carry them in coffins?"

Kam Shar's gray eyes sparkled. "I do. Remember the cartons?"

"I've called them off. They aren't hunting you anymore."

"I'll accept your word for that, although that means your sway isn't supreme."

"What's that supposed to mean?" said Addard.

"I'm still being hunted. If they aren't acting on your orders, I assume it's on someone else's."

"People don't act normally when they're terrified. Tell me, Mr. Alien, can you smell the stink of my metropolis? Does its odor reach your nostrils as you fly overhead via your private mode of transportation? You know, we wingless men don't have it so easy; we're pretty much stuck wherever we happen to be and can't go anywhere. I wonder what we'll do when communications break down?"

"Good-bye, Mr. Mayor. I'll see you soon for the last scene of the drama." Kam Shar extended his own wrist and pressed the hypo to it. Looking up he said, "To show you that I'm in it all the way with you."

After he had gone, Addard sat and watched another speck of blood ooze from the wound in his arm.

Chapter X

Monkwell's normally pink face was more flushed than usual as he spoke on the intercom to Addard. "Don't give me any guff! I want to know what happened with that kid after I left your office!"

"And I'm telling you again that nothing happened."

Mopping his forehead with a handkerchief, Monkwell said, 'Elaborate. Be more specific."

"I don't know how much more specific I can be. Five minutes after you left I sent the boy away."

"You used the truth serum."

"I did not," said Addard. "I turned him loose. I let him go. I did nothing to him."

For a long moment Monkwell was silent. At last he spoke. "Then they did it."

"Who? Did what?"

"Garly and Ennesto. They must have grabbed him again behind your back. The kid is with Roxey now, that blind guy who works most of the time at the airport. The kid, beaten black and blue, was dumped at a clinic and he's in a coma. That isn't all they've done. Roxey told me he was sent by Ennesto to number fifty-two gymnasium, where Kam Shar's bodies were supposedly hidden in an air tunnel. They weren't there. Now they have armed guards everywhere hunting for them. I hear they're pumping gas into all shafts, and I can bet they aren't doing it for the benefit of the Fluger."

"You're right. We already tried gas on him. Okay, leave it to me. I'll take care of them."

"They must be crazy. They were right there in that meeting when we all decided the alien was our only hope." Having vented at least some of his frustration, Monkwell relaxed. Never had he spoken like that to his superior, and they were both surprised. With a frown, he lifted the back of his wrist to his mouth and sucked.

"Has Kam Shar been to see you?" Addard asked.

"Yes. He just left."

"Did he get you with a hypo?"

Monkwell stared at his wrist. "He touched me, but I didn't feel anything. There's a little drop of blood."

"Did he say why? I mean, why did he come?"

"I was wondering that myself. He just said I'd be in on it, that I'd earned a role because I was your adviser. He said that was the way he always did it. What's going on? What was in the hypo?"

Lately, number-three adviser hadn't been sounding as stupid as usual; bewildered, yes, but not idiotic. Perhaps crises brought out Monkwell's best. Those were Addard's thoughts as he rode the cab at a speed slightly faster than a jog. The tunnels between his and his advisers' apartments were supposed to be open and safe. Neither Ennesto nor Garly was answering incoming calls.

"You're fired when this is all over," he said a little while later to Ennesto. He was in the old politician's bedroom where a dozen medics hovered and attempted to appear knowledgeable and useful. "You know that, don't you?" he added.

"What do I care?" shrilled Ennesto. "I'm infested with some kind of foreign thing and you talk to me about a job! I told you to kill that alien as soon as we discovered he was aboard this planet."

"You told me a lot of things and they were all hysterical." For a moment Addard experienced a stab of compassion for his colleague. Every one of Ennesto's ninety-two years was vividly etched on his face as he lay on his bed and allowed the medics to tend him.

"They can't get it out!" he whined. "It's some kind of tape."

"Tape? What kind?"

"I just said some kind, didn't I? How do I know? They

don't know either. They're such elegant idiots! We give them the best educations and all they can do is prescribe physics!"

Addard went into the living room with the head physician and listened attentively. It seemed that the alien, Mr. Kam Shar, the one with all those bodies everyone was searching for, had paid a visit to Mr. Ennesto a short time ago, in his office. The alien had said something about a boy and then stuck Mr. Ennesto with a hypo. The needle had injected a microscopic tape into the old man's bloodstream. All it was doing now was moving around inside the body. It wasn't a difficult process to trace an article of the tape's size with the anatomy scanner, just as it wasn't difficult to predict its course. Sooner or later it would lodge somewhere. Then what? The physician had no idea.

"It will probably settle down within the next few hours," he said. "In one of the organs. Or in a muscle. Maybe in a joint. One place is as good as another for whatever it's going to do."

"How do you know?"

"I'm guessing. Since I assume it was injected into him for a purpose, I also assume it's going to do what it was put in him for. It's giving off a minuscule signal. Not exactly electronic. More like radiant energy such as the brain gives off. It's so slight, though, that we can't be certain. Our instruments are very fine, but this is an inimitable piece of work. Kam Shar knows his onions."

There wasn't anything they could do for Ennesto but tell him what they knew and try to make him comfortable. For his age, he was in good shape, and his life-span ought to be well over a hundred, but these were tough times and many predictions were being thrown out the window. If Ennesto didn't blow his cork he might weather this particular crisis. That is, until the tape in his bloodstream settled somewhere and did something.

"How would you like it if you kept thinking you might explode?" he said.

"I don't like it." The way Addard said it aroused Ennesto's curiosity.

"What do you mean?"

"I mean that Kam Shar also blessed me with an injection."

Ennesto made him elaborate, wanted to know exactly what

occurred, every little detail. When Addard was finished, the old man seemed a bit more relaxed. It obviously made him feel better to know his condition was shared.

"Could it be a bomb?" he asked. The physician only shrugged.

"It could be anything, though if Kam Shar wanted to blow you up, I should have thought he'd simply drop explosives on you. If he used compressed molecules, there could be an enormous amount of material inside that tape."

"He's an alien," the old man said. "How do we know how aliens think?" Nobody responded to his words and he began whining. To Addard he said, "You think I hit that boy again, but you're wrong. Garly beat him up, acted like a maniac, slugged him until he threw up. Kept doing it too, even after the youngster told him everything."

"And when I get to Garly and ask him, he's going to tell me you did it. No wonder Kam Shar shot us all with the same bullet."

Too exhausted to argue, Ennesto said, "I hope he got Garly. Would he do it just because of one kid?"

"He might, though I don't think it's the answer. That was just coincidental, but he got us all, so it's a moot point."

Garly was all for stepping up the hunt.

"Which hunt?" Addard wanted to know. "For the Fluger?"

"No!" The short man's response was more like a snarl. Tugging on his thin mustache, he sat at his office desk and looked angry. "That can wait."

"I think not. Wendelar from Superior and all the other mayors are waiting for us to dispose of the problem."

"They won't do anything. What do you think they are, savages?"

"They won't want to do anything, although if they see us going under, they're liable to decide to finish the burial rather than risk having the Fluger snoop around and find them. One bomb should take care of him."

"We had him outside once. We could have bombed him ourselves."

"And you and Ennesto sent tanks after him."

"How was I supposed to know he had hide like fifty feet

of steel?" Garly pulled on his mustache too hard, winced. His thin face was pale, his expression harsh. "Never mind that. We can put every available man into the hunt."

"No. They're going to continue trying to hold the city together."

Garly seemed not to hear. "You say he did the same thing to himself? Injected his own arm? I find that hard to believe. It was probably sham."

"It was as genuine as ours. We might as well stop trying to find answers ahead of time."

With a sneer, the other said, "You mean we'll know soon enough? Do you really expect me to sit around and wait?"

"Yes, because if you don't, I'll regard you as a common criminal and have you locked up. I hope you take me seriously. If you want to conduct a clandestine search for Kam Shar with a reasonably small group, I'll not object. Anything on a larger scale will make me move against you. I want him whole and unharmed."

Someone tried to poison the reservoir where the Fluger went to drink nearly every day. It didn't work because the reservoir was too large, besides which the perpetrator was caught and taken to jail before the attempt could succeed. It never could have succeeded. Poison couldn't hurt the enemy.

The incident served to cause the government to again urge people not to use reservoir water being pumped into the small dispensers in their apartments. They could walk to the nearest kitchen and pick up enough in containers to see them through the day.

Addard decided to have crews pick up fresh produce from the garden areas and distribute it on the walkways where people could easily reach it. He received the shock of his life when he went next door to his fourth adviser's office to give the order.

She was sitting on the couch with a big, black, four-legged animal. His head lay in her lap and she stroked him with a gentle hand. Or was it a fond hand? Addard was too angry to make the distinction.

"Half the city is hunting for him, and you've got him on your lap like a dog," he said, immediately regretting his tone.

Kam Shar arose from his casual position, yawned, stretched and loped away at a leisurely pace.

Meanwhile, Addard pondered his next move. Should he tell her the alien didn't think much of him and might think nothing of stabbing him in the back? Should he mention that he cared more for her than he had let on?

"Nobody's going out these days, so we'll have to deliver food closer to the apartments in the areas where the kitchens aren't functioning," he said. "Get word to the farmers, will you? If they need help they can get it from the police."

The airport in Section One was besieged by mobs wanting out. Roxey helped supervise the cleaning of the runways, while scores of policemen kept the crowd behind ropes back of the planes. Driving a tractor with a grader on the back, he mostly sat on the sidelines and marveled that people would be so anxious to fly into the unknown. Of course, the fact that the Fluger was wreaking havoc just one section over had a deal to do with the bedlam.

An exhausted helicopter pilot sat in his craft beside the tractor. Young and red-eyed from lack of sleep, he sprawled in the seat and kept shaking his head. "They think they're going to Superior or one of the other cities. Why don't they have better sense?"

"Maybe they know and don't care," said Roxey.

At first Wendelar and the other mayors had accepted a few refugees, until the idea occurred to them that the Fluger might stow away on one of the planes. No matter how earnestly they were assured that the alien creature was too large to hide on a cruiser or copter, they remained unconvinced and closed their ports to Olympian ships. Now the pilots of the plagued metropolis were taking their passengers to slum towns and either coaxing or bullying them to disembark.

"I don't know what they expect me to do," Roxey said. "I'm supposed to see that the cargo in the sheds gets dumped into the ocean. How do I do it without planes?"

"What's the cargo?"

"You must have just come on duty this morning."

"I did."

"Dead bodies. We quit trying to bury them all."

104

Most of the day Roxey scraped runways and monitored the crowd as it gradually diminished, not because the planes were handling them all but because word had filtered in that the Fluger was moving east.

The young pilot was in the last group to go out and invited the blind man to go along and help him keep order. They touched down somewhere in Pennsylvania, which frightened the passengers who had either hoped or expected to be taken to a civilized city.

"Do you want to go back?" said Roxey, holding the door open for them. "You can, you know. We aren't kicking you out. The whole trip was your idea."

The town was ancient and dilapidated, dirty and somehow hollow looking. Its empty windows were mouths that told of past glories. Nobody on the plane would have believed any of those stories. The passengers were from the future, which for some reason had always been painted brighter than the present or the past.

"Make up your minds, said the pilot. "You can get along in this town if you work."

"I'm not going back to Olympus," said a woman. "I lived in constant fear for my life. Maybe I'll do the same thing here but I won't have a monster dogging my tracks." She stepped past Roxey, climbed down the ladder, slowly walked toward the nearest building. One by one the rest followed.

"They should put signs everywhere in Olympus telling people what to expect out here," said Roxey.

"What can they expect? Hunger and wolves? You can't tell the truth all the time."

They returned to the airport, where Roxey saw to his crew. Most of them had gone home. The crowd was still large, but night flights were forbidden by the government so eventually the area cleared.

Stopping at a kitchen in an untouched boulevard, he bought his dinner and then found a cab that took him home. As soon as he walked into the apartment he knew something was different. It was in the air, a gross vacancy filtering through the rooms and reminding him of another sense of loss he had experienced years before.

Hulian was gone, plucked up like a pebble or a shell on a

beach. The cords on the feeding bottles hung uselessly over the bed bars, the rumpled pillow and sheets were askew, the robe and slippers lay on a chair, the oxygen mask was on the floor. The boy had been dying and now he was gone.

The first thing he saw when he opened his eyes was a mirror. Maybe it had been placed in front of him so he could see the hole in his head above the outer corner of his right eyebrow. Just at the hairline and the size of a dime, it was very definitely a hole. It didn't ooze, which amazed him, as he had always supposed his skull to be filled with brains.

A hand came into view to paste a bandage across it. That was the next thing he saw upon awakening. Then he noticed the eyes, gray, sparkling, full of emotions that other humans didn't seem to see. He relaxed. He was with a friend.

The shaft was equipped with a portable lamp, air-conditioner, food and water dispensers, toilet, a small hospital and more than enough platforms to support Kam Shar's bodies. The black animal lay to Hulian's right, near enough so that he could reach out and stroke it, while the winged one lay prone on an upper tier.

The vacuums overhead had been turned off, and all gas pipes were plugged. Several meters away was a tiny shard of sunlight that came through an opening to the outside. He imagined he could smell the spring burgeoning in his old part of the world. Self-pity welled in him, and along with it came a violent surge of homesickness. Oh, for the days of poverty, peace and a loving old man who told him sweet lies.

Clutching the hand of an alien born trillions of miles away, he hid his face in the bare mattress provided for him and shed some tears. He was ashamed that a foreigner had to take time out from his business to do for him what his own kind couldn't or wouldn't. Then he thought of the big, gruff blind man who loved him and his feeling of shame increased. That gave him more to cry about, so he blubbered heartily and felt better for it. With his mixed-up eyes on the pale white face of the man from the stars, he lay still and soon fell asleep.

He was alone when he awakened with the sensation that several days had passed. The bandage on his head was gone. The wound was closed but tender. Kam Shar was absent. The black animal still lay inertly in its place but the winged one had flown away, while on a nearby platform lay the humanoid body.

After giving himself a sponge bath, Hulian had a small breakfast and then snooped in Kam Shar's things. It didn't bother his conscience since he assumed that Eldoron had locked up whatever he wished to keep private.

A box of strange items earned his fascination, small and intricate objects that took him a long time to identify. At last he realized they were weapons. There were little pellets and darts to be propelled by a tiny slingshot so heavy he could scarcely pick it up, arrows waited to be fitted into an odd and dangerous bow that made the ammo fly backward toward the archer before suddenly hurtling forward. The bow wasn't as heavy as the slingshot, but it was still so cumbersome that he failed to shoot himself when he tried it out.

There were tubes that silently sent sharp missiles deep into the wooden beams of the shaft. In fact, one or two went all the way through and disappeared into the wall. Several tubes were fastened so tightly he couldn't get them open.

Kam Shar hadn't brought much clothing from Eldoron, a few black shirts and trousers, soft shoes made of an unidentifiable material, some cloaks. In the carton with the clothes were a transparent vial of tiny feathers, a lock of curly fur and another wisp of softer hair.

While he was looking at the vial and its contents, Kam Shar flew into the opening in the far wall and walked across the beams. "Those belong to my daughter," he said. "She was born not long ago."

"We carry pictures," said Hulian. "Photographs."

"I know. As long as I have something of hers I can see her. I think a photograph might be simpler but it's the human way."

"You mean you can really see her as long as you carry this tube?"

"In my mind, yes."

"But you can't show her to anyone."

"We would never do that, anyway."

During the next few days the Eldoron showed him how the fastened tubes worked. Opening one, he pointed it at a beam and pressed the top, whereupon a yellow ring of light encompassed a centimeter of the wood. Nothing happened, though

Hulian watched for a while. Then, when he shrugged and scowled, Kam Shar laughed.

For three days Hulian kept checking on the ring of light to make certain it was still there.

One afternoon Kam Shar did a strange thing, walked over to a low, horizontal beam, stood with his back to it and draped his wings over it. Suddenly he went limp. Almost simultaneously the humanoid body on the platform stirred and stood on its feet.

Kam Shar dressed in Earth clothes, slacks and sweater, socks and canvas shoes, slipped two brown discs over his irises to hide their glittering gray. Hulian was astonished to see that he looked completely human.

Before they climbed up out of the shaft the boy looked back at the patch of light on the beam. Even as he stared at it, it slowly faded, and in another moment there was nothing to indicate it had existed. For days it had been there and now it was gone. For the first time in days, he smiled.

A short time later they stood in an el suspended high above the main reservoir and watched the Fluger have his daily bath. There were other els hugging the walls, some with people in them, fascinated or benumbed humans drawn to view what might represent the end of their reality. The Fluger never looked up at them but even if he had he could never jump so high. Olympians were learning about their enemy. He was able to leap no more than ten and a half meters straight up into the air, though he could climb a vertical wall. However, if he decided to go after one of the els, it could outrun him to the ceiling, and its passengers might climb through the vents and ride another to the floor or across the ceiling of the next room. Of course, the predator might rip a hole in the wall at any spot, conceivably catch the riders on their way down the other side, but no one anticipated any such act of aggression at the present. It was common knowledge that the alien grew bored with the carnage he created, had even gotten so lax that on various occasions people had actually been quite near him and lived to tell about it.

"Why can't they poison the water?" asked Hulian. He and Kam Shar were the sole occupants of an el resting squarely in the middle of the ceiling.

"It wouldn't work. You can do it with a small body of water but not with something of this size. Half the populace would die if they tried it. Besides, poison won't hurt him."

"What about a really sharp arrow shot from a catapult?"

"His skin is never still. It ripples and flows like an ocean. Anything touching it is carried elsewhere. It's like the sheets of magnitum on the roof that bring the light down into the city."

"You mean it's that fast?" said Hulian.

"Not quite, but you can't kill him by shooting him."

"What about fire?"

"His world is practically made of fire. It's full of lightning, intense pressure and all the other elements that harm people like us."

"Are you telling me he can't be killed?"

"No, he isn't indestructible."

"Then what? What can kill him?"

"I can."

"When?"

"It has already begun. We wait now for him to sleep. It will be soon. Once a year or every three hundred and seventy-two Earth days he sleeps."

"Once a year! How long does he stay asleep?"

"Seven of your days."

"Then we will kill him while he's helpless?"

"No, after he awakens."

"He'll be sluggish? Weak?"

"He will be at his most ferocious."

Chapter XI

During the trip from Fluga, Corradado had sensed the death that awaited him outside the stowaway craft, so he remained in hiding, hadn't ripped his way through the crew and the steel partitions to get to freedom and bitter darkness. Now and then he recalled that strange trip, not fully comprehending its complexity but aware that he had gone away from his home and traveled a far distance in the sky. How he would return when the notion captured him wasn't a problem in his mind. He only knew that when the time came, he would.

Not entirely ignorant, he realized the shriekers had wanted to send him home that day not long ago when they presented him with a free and uncluttered passage through sections of the city straight to a vehicle similar to the one that brought him from Fluga. Unfortunately for Olympus, he hadn't been ready to leave, so he tore a hole in the side of the ship, which had been wired to explode in outer space, and killed the shriekers in the area. When it was time to return home, he would go out of this stinking metropolis, walk across the land outside, staying under the sky for an appropriate length of time, and eventually he would arrive at his destination.

While he drank from the water of the reservoir and thought of the past, his attention was attracted by something in the depths. Forty meters or so downward a shrieker drifted and took photographs of him with a camera.

The shrieker reacted in a panicked fashion as the big creature dove in and came plowing down after him, dropped his camera and swam toward a screened partition in a concrete wall of the reservoir. Sinking was easier for the Fluger than boring through solid rock and doing without oxygen didn't bother him at all. As for the pressure, there wasn't any to speak of for him.

Just as the human reached the screen and frantically tried to open it, Corradado took a foot in his jaws, walked across the bottom and climbed up the wall to the surface, the trip taking him approximately two minutes. Tossing his victim onto the concrete walk he utilized a single blow of his right forepaw to rip away the front of the rubber suit. Also torn off were the man's face, chest and abdominal flesh, so that the warm internals were exposed for easy feeding. While people in els high above the scene gagged or watched in silence, the creature from the stars dined, leaving nothing but the rubber suit.

Feeling more sluggish than he usually did after eating, he lay down and considered the fact that soon he would need to have his annual sleep. He must find a suitable spot, a place of darkness, quiet and solitude, one where no enemy could reach him in a week's time.

He possessed more than a primitive consciousness regarding human ingenuity, knew they had tools that could bore, blast, crush, sift, dig, etc. Still, working with tools took time; all he had to do was choose his sleeping hole in secret.

Had it not been for his innate savagery, he still would have destroyed Olympus. He hated its symmetry and huge dimensions, its smells, sounds and sensations, but most of all he detested its inhabitants.

Never had he been able to vent so much rage as he had since coming here. Whenever he tried tearing things up on Fluga, some adult came along and knocked him about, beat his ears flat, strapped his rear with his paws, kicked him whimpering and wailing into an abyss. He hoped it wasn't a fact of nature with his kind that maturing meant a slowing down or a mellowing of the individual. Anyway, here in Olympus there was no one who stood up to him, with the exception of the odd one, who even now stood in a cage in the center of the ceiling observing him.

He looked up and snarled, causing several shriekers to gasp and move nervously about in their cages, but the odd one made no response at all. The Fluger liked this one. He was different,

111

had courage, resources, aplomb, an interesting manner. Killing him would be enjoyable.

What would it be like to destroy a world? Such a thought made the creature uneasy, for he caught flashes of visions in his head of a glowing ball in the sky that represented the place where the shriekers lived. If they and he were on that glowing ball in an ocean of blackness, where was Fluga and how would he get there?

No matter, he would get home. In the meantime, how would it be to turn this globe upside down, or what would it feel like to rip a hole through it? Perhaps he wasted his good times by remaining in this place. It stood to reason there were other things on the ball besides Olympus.

Flexing his claws, he snorted and stretched, bulged his muscles, unknowingly horrified the onlookers. Rising, he leisurely walked from the reservoir complex and went off to have his exercise. Work crews in Section Two, Boulevard Nineteen, were trying to repair a northside wall that had a gaping hole in it, and when he burst, snarling and hostile, through the archway, everyone dropped what he was doing and ran. The daylight coming in the hole interested Corradado more than the fleeing humans, who were innumerable and always handy anyway. Instead of chasing the workers, he went to investigate the damage he had done several days previously.

The wall around the opening seemed to have weakened, perhaps because he had given it such a strong kick directly in the center, where the plastic, plaster, wood and steel appeared to be the most densely concentrated. Or perhaps the construction had been inferior in this one spot in the first place. For whatever reason, the Fluger experienced a sense of power as he kicked the northwestern side of the wall and heard a loud splitting sound. He couldn't be certain, but he believed the floor beneath him trembled. Racing to the northeastern part of the wall, he turned and kicked it with both back feet, after which he sped to the southeastern archway and whirled to watch what happened.

If there hadn't been especially thick beams at the eastern and western edges of the boulevard, the splitting might have gone on and on. As it was, those edges broke wide open so that the wall simply fell out of Olympus, dropped straight away and took some upper apartments with it. Where the floors were weak above the wall the apartments fell, their ceilings ripping and causing still higher apartments to collapse.

While he moved across the section kicking out walls, a single el moved across the ceilings with him. Waiting until he was close to an archway, which meant the two passengers above him would by then have transferred to another machine on the other side of the partition, he leaped up and planted his paws flat in a vertical-climb position.

Up the wall he went and made a hole at the spot where he hoped the next el might even then be beginning to move. Angered, he stuck his head through and watched as the machine rode to the ground. He remembered that he had done this before. If he ran down the wall, the odd one would transfer to another el going up the other side. He wasn't swift and agile enough to catch this enemy.

The longing to crush the odd one between his jaws made his throat ache. Reluctantly, he turned to go back down his side of the wall, changed his mind and crossed the ceiling to a large screened vent leading to the outside. Clawing his way to freedom, he walked up the looping O to the top of Olympus, chose a comfortable spot and lay down to sunbathe.

For some reason, he didn't mind the height, liked being up there, enjoyed the view from this highest point of the city, fancied himself as king of all he surveyed, which didn't seem to be a great deal, unfortunately. One city and grass plains didn't a fabulous kingdom make, though on a clear day such as today he imagined he saw something in the distance that would be worth investigating when he grew bored with Olympus. His telescopic vision wasn't infallible by any means; the distant image might be a shadow or a mirage.

It was several hours later that he retreated into the inner city to chase and catch his lunch. He was angered anew to discover that the odd one waited for him in an el at floor level, prepared to go in either direction.

That was the pattern all day. No matter where he went the odd one kept pace with him, staying just beyond reach.

The mayor of Superior was a big, heavy woman with thick blond hair and dark brown eyes. She wore the uniform of the day, green overalls and green shirt. At the moment, she was offended by fate and circumstance, having believed her city's security unbreachable by anyone from Olympus or anywhere else.

Feigning patience and tolerance, she listened to what the alien named Kam Shar had to say. When he was finished, she told her people to lock him up. He certainly looked human, and as far as she was concerned he might as well be treated like anybody else. And he surely had gall, considering the proposals he made to her.

She wasn't happy about what she had done. He couldn't very well be killing the Fluger in Olympus while he sat in one of her jails.

That evening the guards summoned her to the cell and together they examined the hole in the wall. Kam Shar was gone. He had escaped by using either a small amount of explosive or some corrosive but controlled acid. Whatever he had done, he was very neat about it, left a smooth round aperture a meter in diameter.

It must have been acid, since no one in the area heard an explosion. Of course, the Eldoron had been searched before being locked away. Out of sorts and disturbed, Wendelar tried to figure out why the visitor from afar had come in the first place if he intended to leave so soon. It was annoying of him to show her how easily he could get out.

He was in her apartment when she awakened the next morning, sitting in her living room watching a *tev* program about teaching techniques.

"It was easy," he said to her. "I spiritually abandoned the cell and entered my winged body, which was hidden in a slum town a few kilometers distant. Flying here to Superior, I made my way to the compartment adjoining the cell, burned a hole in the wall with an instrument I happened to be carrying with me, carried away the humanoid body and flew back to the slum town."

"You expect me to believe that?" Still in her nightgown, Wendelar looked worried.

"You do believe it. You know practically everything that goes on in Olympus, and I made certain you received photographs and *tev* images of my three forms. You know exactly who and what I am, why I'm on Kappa and why I'm in this room in your city."

"You can't threaten me."

"Threats are only words and anyone can speak them."

Wendelar went to a wall switch and flipped it. There should have been a soft beeping sound as guards were summoned. Nothing happened. "What, what?" she said.

Kam Shar had returned his attention to the *tev*. "This is the only thing I didn't turn off. It's an interesting program."

Wendelar went about the apartment trying to turn something on, but nothing worked, not even the front archway. No matter how many times she stood in the middle of the living room and walked toward the blank panel it didn't slide back. The intercom was dead, the timepieces were stalled, the food and water dispensers failed to function.

"How did you do it?" she said to her guest.

"Special tools from Eldoron. Very fine, very advanced."

"And you think you can do the same thing to the entire city of Superior?"

"It will take a century to put it back in its present condition if I turn it off. Incidentally, you'll have to find another apartment. This one is ruined. When we leave we'll have to go through a hole in the wall."

"I could bomb Olympus while you're in it. That would take care of the Fluger and all three of you."

"I checked out their warning systems. I'd have at least three minutes and I assure you that would give me plenty of time to escape."

"From that kind of explosion?" said Wendelar with a frown. "You couldn't possibly fly far enough."

"High enough, though."

Pensive, disgruntled and apparently afflicted with a touch of indigestion, the mayor began to pace. "Why don't I just kill you right now?"

"You would only be destroying one of my forms, an act that would annoy me to an intense degree. Besides, what are you going to kill me with?"

She took a handgun from a bookshelf, aimed it at the floor and pulled the trigger. It failed to fire, and she returned it to the shelf. "That's uncanny. Are all alien civilizations superior to Earth's?"

"I don't know, I haven't seen them all."

"Modesty? For a while I believed there wasn't anything you didn't know. Anyhow, I don't think you're as much the wizard as you'd like me to imagine. In my opinion, you've used some kind of electronic damping field."

"You could call it that, although molecular stunning would be more accurate. Don't expect the things in this apartment to function again for at least a decade. If you're still around then, you can experience the spectacle of seeing and hearing everything start to work simultaneously."

"Joy, pleasure."

"About the evacuation of Sections Eight to Ten, I wouldn't delay it. If the Fluger decides to head that way again I'm afraid he might succeed in getting in, no matter how many bodies pile up in front of him."

"Ugh, oh, what a mess!" she said.

"Only seeing is believing and you haven't seen."

"Let me cover the ground rules, since I don't want to miss anything. We're to open enough underground cab tunnels to take out the people in those three sections and we're to open other tunnels to carry away their sludge and garbage. Anything else?"

"I'll let you know."

"I'm sure."

A more surreptitious maneuver than the evacuation of the children's sections in Olympus had never been carried out in Roxey's memory. By the millions, approximately six million to be exact, they sneaked or were carried by sneaking adults down the long length of the eastern pillar, from there entering cabs that took them through kilometers of earth to safety in Superior. For the first time in the city's history the citizens benefited all the way because of its advanced automation. The three hundred els in the sections to be evacuated could carry ten to eleven adults—more than three thousand passengers each trip. If nothing happened, if the Fluger stayed away and there were no major breakdowns of equipment, the evacuation should be completed in forty-five days. The word had come from the mayor's office that they wouldn't have to finish the evacuation since the Fluger would be

116

killed within a matter of hours, or days. Meanwhile, they were to hurry with all facility.

It was only the first day and Roxey had already exhausted himself searching for Hulian in the crowds riding els and cabs. There were many youths fitting his description; only true eyesight could have discerned whether or not a specific person was his young friend. After accosting at least a hundred boys of certain height, weight, cast of features and tight curls of hair, he gave up and concentrated on his job. What made him think Hulian wasn't lying somewhere dead? Secretly he hoped. The boy had surely been kidnapped by Kam Shar, who had the medical knowledge to give him a new eye. Maybe the alien had other knowledge, such as how to relieve the pressure of brain swell.

The evacuation continued on through the night hours, but Roxey quit about midnight and staggered home. He lay in his bed in the empty apartment and listened to the silence. His hearing unit rested in a drawer, so he felt completely normal. All over the city people were staring into utter darkness just as he was doing. Stretching, he felt his feet stick out from under the cover. Olympus had the finest things technology could give but it didn't know how to make a bed long enough for a big man.

He fell asleep and dreamed of the things he had seen and done that day. Again he ushered people into els, listened to the crying of infants. Children lost their nannies and had to be taken in tow by strangers, anxious parents refused to get on the els until their strays were rounded up, ambulances were parked in front of the cages to unload the sick and injured. There was bedlam of a sort and yet the atmosphere was one of furtive haste and vast relief. How much more fortunate were they than other Olympians forced to stay while the Fluger moved among them, consuming ten or fifteen of them and murdering hundreds each day.

The underground tunnels were clogged, yet each cab that came along managed to take away a full complement. The automation of Olympus was paying off.

In other tunnels cabs were dumping their foul loads into trucks that took them outside, kilometers away, and left them, not in an old dumping ground but in an untouched place. It wasn't polluted out there because the nuclear furnaces in Olympus burned nearly everything, just as they would burn it again once the Fluger was out of the way. For now, the pipes and vents were closed off and in a state of repair, while the wilderness of the eastern continent took the city's trash and buried it under vines and brush.

Roxey found the letter the next morning after he dressed and fastened his unit into place. It was in the mailbox in his living room. Someone had dropped it in the slot during the night.

Though he pored over it with his unit working at full capacity, he couldn't read a single word of it. A friend read it to him while they had breakfast in a nearby kitchen.

"Dear Roxey,

I'm okay. Naturally I'm not writing this letter since I'm illiterate (you'll take care of that after the trouble is over, won't you? I mean, send me to school?). You-Know-Who has fixed me all up. I think he's a doctor when he's on his own planet, which can't be often since he tells me he takes one offworld job after another. He does it because he's a fiddlefoot. I think I'm one, too, because I wouldn't mind taking off with him, but he has a policy of keeping his hands off everything and everybody that he can. That means he won't take me.

"I have a hole in my head that's ugly but it's healing fast. That and my eyes make me especially homely, though I've yet to have anyone faint at sight of me. I have the job of trailing the Fluger, while Kam Shar carries on in other battlefields. (That's his comment.) It isn't a dangerous job, since he showed me how to stay out of the Fluger's reach. He says it's particularly important that I don't lose sight of that big killer because it's about to find itself a place to take a week-long nap. If we don't kill it right after it wakes up we have to wait another year, unless Kam Shar tosses it a haphazard bone, which is against his principles. (I don't know what he means by that.)

"He's secretive and his ways are different from ours so on specific points there can sometimes be a little fog. I personally believe that's just an excuse he uses when he

118

doesn't want to answer my questions. He has a brother who cares for his six-year-old daughter. His wife was killed.

"Regarding my eyes, he isn't color-blind at all; he did it deliberately so that I would stand out from my fellow man. He learned much about Earth before coming but neglected to notice how much we hate being regarded as freaks, says he'll be happy to change my blue one for a brown but for some reason I've grown fond of it. If I give it up it will be like giving up a part of him I admire. So I've decided to keep my crazy eyes the way they are. And they do make me stand out from my fellow man.

"Regarding his bodies, he says he has been killed many times but he's okay as long as he has a final moment or two to switch his spirit to one of the other forms. Naturally all three of them haven't been killed at once otherwise he wouldn't be here writing this letter for me. Whenever one of his bodies is destroyed on a job he waits until he gets home and then has another grown from one of his cells which is fertilized by one of his special chromosomes. (I assume you understand that.)

"I'm taking you at your word that you want me to be your son. I'm not going back to the outside, and Kam Shar won't have me, so I'm going to need you. Maybe one day I'll be able to pay you back. Don't worry about me and I'll see you soon.

Old blue-brown eyes.

P.S. He says he isn't a doctor. He's a judge."

Chapter XII

Quantro Tilzer had been trying to get out of Olympus ever since the day Kam Shar took him away from the slum people and brought him back to his old apartment by the junk pile.

Had the Eldoron left him in that particular spot to show him how well acquainted he was with his life-style? All the barber really knew was that his days were numbered as long as he remained within the city walls.

He stayed in the apartment just one night, long enough to learn that the Fluger still made a nesting ground out of the mess behind the building. Surely the government was made up of a bunch of fools. The domiciles along the block had been repaired but the pile of debris was left untouched. Didn't the idiots realize how close this area was to the main reservoir where the yellow murderer went every day? The entire section ought to be cordoned off. Citizens should be warned.

He called the police before moving out, but when he went back a few days later the pile was still there. The alley was in the shade though the crooked light of high noon showered the boulevard. It reminded him of the cemetery where he had buried his mother. It was quiet there, too, and just as saturated with silent pain and unspoken promises. She had hated what he was.

His new apartment was closer to the salon, much more respectable, cleaner; a few customers actually came by now and then. It seemed that one must still have one's locks shorn, shaped or discolored even when there was a good chance that mutilation and death lay around the corner.

The apartment was too tidy. It made him feel cluttered.

Also it was too comfortable for a man who had every intention of making tracks just as soon as an opportunity presented itself.

Daily he rode cabs or walked to the western pillar to see if he could bum a ride on something going south, but the work crews seemed to know he didn't belong and chased him away no matter how he was dressed. They treated him with disrespect.

"Don't hang around here," they said. "You'll not ride in this cab. Can't you see we're doing what we can to save something for the future? You're in the way and don't tell us you're on the job. Do you think we can't smell the booze and the pomade, and do you think we can't see your lily-white palms? Not a callus on 'em, though we suspect your backside's plastered with big ones. Vamoose before we dump you down a shaft."

There were all kinds of entrances into the pillar but none was so unoccupied that he could get to the bottom where he might sneak outside and make his way to a slum town. Or perhaps he would just live out in the open with the coyotes, like an aborigine of old. There were millions of places out there where he would be safe from an alien afflicted with a giant case of megalomania.

"All you have to do is perform the rituals and repeat the chants," he said to the young man who had come into the salon. He set down his cup of tea. Sick of the stuff, he hadn't drunk any, though the customer sucked his to the final dreg. "Sit down and memorize what's written on the paper."

"Why can't I take it with me?"

For some reason the man's features appeared blurred to Quantro. He looked like a hundred other young fellows with whom he had done business. Or a thousand. "Are you a hound?" he asked.

That amused the other. "There isn't enough money in police work. Even if there were and even if I happened to be a lieutenant or even a chief, I'd desert these days. Those guys have to make meals of themselves whenever the UKO comes around, stand out in front of ordinary citizens like cheesecakes or pot roasts. I mean, can you imagine trying to get a cannibalistic monster to settle for your meat so he won't try to sample your neighbor's?"

"I can imagine it but I don't intend to do it," said Quantro.

"Nor I. I've a bad memory and it'll take me a while to learn all this."

"So sit and do it."

"What if I meet the Fluger on the way home?"

"Project, man. Fly over him."

"That may be easy enough to do with what's inside this body but what about the body itself?"

"What do you think you bought with your money? I'm not selling immortality, you know."

"Still I wonder what would happen to my spirit if my body met with an accident while I was projecting."

He was an imbecile and Quantro didn't give him a second thought after he left. Not one to lull himself into pretending no danger was present when it walked around with him like a companion in an invisible shroud, he continued riding back to the pillar entrances every morning. Having already tried the airport, he knew thousands were being flown out during daylight hours, but just let him try and get close enough to become a passenger. The mobs were made up of surly curs who thought nothing of bashing heads to make the lines shorter in front of them. No, the best way was down one of the els or in a cab that rode the declines.

If he'd had any friends he would have imposed upon them, but only if they lived in a quiet area where danger didn't threaten. While he wondered why most of the universe seemed to possess some sort of sanctuary when he had none, he remembered that there was somebody after all. Should he call her friend? Acquaintance? Used-to-know? He decided to go and see.

It had been years since he came this way and he was surprised to see the flowers growing in boxes in front of the place, taken aback to notice how brazenly the nameplate stood out on the cornerpiece of the apartment. Somehow his imagination had grown a tombstone in this spot, an old and graying monument representing the colorless years he had once spent here. And the years he had been away. He had killed them, in a manner of speaking, so why weren't they dead and why weren't their graves weedstrewn and neglected?

She answered his ring and he was shocked because she hadn't changed at all. Still patient, yet endowed with x-ray vision, she let him in. He received another shock when he saw a younger version of himself sitting at a piano composing, concentrating, cool, detached, uncaring. Where in his lineage was there a penchant for music that his only issue should end up a player of tunes?

He didn't linger. The years of separation were a tombstone after all, covering his jabs and digs with unconcern. They were immune. His ability to wound was no longer keen. Like everyone they feared the Fluger, were fortunate that the beast hadn't touched their level. Yes, everything was fine with them, economically and every other way (particularly now that he wasn't steering their boat) and naturally they hoped he was also fine. They wished him well and hurried him to the exit.

A day later and early in the morning he walked down a corridor between several els, stopped beside one as it opened. A man supervising a load of crates stuck his head out to see if there was more merchandise to be loaded on. At that moment Quantro brought his walking cane down on the unsuspecting skull, hauled the limp form on out of the car and took himself all the way to the bottom of the pillar.

Down below it was havoc, but at least no one cared if he had calluses on his palms or grit in his backbone. It was all he could do to make headway along the corridors between cab tunnels and el shafts.

Convinced that everything and everybody were being transported to slum towns and wilderness, he gave up trying to find any cut-and-dried security and entered a tunnel. Squeezing into a cab filled with crates of rotten oranges, he settled back and tried to relax. He had a pistol and some ammunition, the clothes on his back and a desire to live to be a hundred.

In order to carry away some of Olympus' garbage Wendelar had ordered the blockaded tunnels opened. Since incoming freight practically always consisted of goods the city intended to keep and use, there were only a few small exits to the outside. Consequently, Olympus' trash had to be brought into Superior's western pillar before it could be taken out again to the wilderness.

Quantro knew the difference between ordinary underground cab tunnels and the kind built in a city proper, so when the fancier light shades began playing off the walls and when the

123

stations began to take on a look of elegance his curiosity started to stir. He knew they were nowhere near Olympus—and in fact that metropolis had to be six or seven hundred kilometers behind—yet the smelly cab was periodically passing stations plainly intended for the use of people.

The thought of Superior never entered his head until he leaped from the slowing vehicle and ran up the stairs of the nearest compartment.

Filled with sick anticipation, he fully expected to see the crest of his hometown superimposed upon the grille of the ticket cage. Instead he experienced jubilation and exultation when he saw the silver little moon planted there. No star. A moon! This was Superior! Instead of facing wolves, he was confronted with the plushness of the world's second most famous structure!

There was nothing for him to do but knock the ticket seller on the head and help himself to the cash in the drawer. Alone in a city with which he wasn't overly familiar, he had to have funds, and there was no one about to protest or try to stop him.

Ravenous, he took els to the lowest level of the upper tiers, headed for the nearest kitchen and bought a big breakfast. Finding an empty table, he relaxed and filled his belly. Now and then he silently congratulated himself on his good fortune. No Fluger, no Eldoron, no wife and son. All at once he frowned. No citizenship, either. He would have to be super cautious or Superior would snag him and kick him out. Or would they? Hold on! Of course they wouldn't. They were willingly taking in Olympus' kids, parents, teachers and nannies so why wouldn't they take in a single, clean adult? Glumly he finished his meal. He had made a mistake when he robbed the ticket seller. Now if the police found him they would throw him in jail.

There wasn't that much difference in the layouts of the two cities. Aware that there were sections of apartments into which people could move at almost any time, he rode about on els and in cabs until he located one. What a relief it was to travel without worrying about something huge and hungry coming through a wall to rend one's flesh. How peaceful it was to know one was surrounded on every side by tolerance.

The row of apartments was nearly empty. All he did was

tuck sufficient money into the appropriate slot in the front of his chosen domicile and the panel slid aside to become a door with a tapping code written on a slip of paper.

For the moment he was safe. Eventually he would have to record his name and other particulars on a card and drop it in the slot which had accepted his money. What to do about that? He didn't know. He would worry about it later. In the meantime he could spend the rest of the day drinking and watching *tev*.

Garly considered having his left hand severed but he was too squeamish to do more than talk about it.

"You're crazy even to think such a thing," said Ennesto.

"Don't lie to me. If your tape were in your hand you'd whack it off with a butcher knife."

Ennesto's tape was embedded in his liver. "Possibly. In case you change your mind, though, give it further thought. You might relinquish your appendage only to discover that while the medic was anesthetizing you the tape had moved into your bloodstream and went elsewhere."

"It's almost worth thinking about. I've been reading up on compressed molecules."

"What did you find out?"

"Do you know you can stick a cabload of jello on the head of a match?"

"That much?" Ennesto was still in bed and being tended to by medics who looked as if they wished he would either go to sleep or die in a hurry. "Look at the help we get these days," he said. Then to an orderly he snapped, "Mind how you administer my capsules or you'll find yourself out of a job."

Unable to tolerate the old man for more than brief periods of time, Garly left and went to hunt up his wife. She was always hiding from him these days, as if he had grown fangs or developed some disease. As usual, she was with her mother and wouldn't come out of the apartment, though he threw things at the front panel and made incessant calls on his intercom. Her mother had practically sold her to him but now was helping her to stay away from him.

"I know she's only eighteen," he said when the mother finally answered his call. "She's been only eighteen all year, and why didn't that matter to you when I handed you the money?"

"She said she loved you is why I did it, not for any money."

Garly could picture her in his mind, blonde, hungry looking, aggravating. Surely his Cili hadn't come from this woman. "No matter why you made the bargain with me, you did make it and now I expect you to stick to it. I'm in trouble and want you to send her out."

"What kind of trouble?"

"What difference does it make? I'm her husband."

"She's talking about divorce."

Garly angrily stroked his mustache. "She won't get one as long as I provide you with funds every month. You won't let her."

"She won't come out. No use your calling or throwing trash at the place. Why don't you just forget the whole thing and go find a wife nearer your own age?"

"I already have a wife." Tired and disgusted, Garly gave up and went to see a Security scientist at a lab on the next boulevard.

"Whoever mentioned compressed molecules was probably way off base," said the man. "Everyone always assumes that people from outer space are smarter than we are but that can't be true. Can't be. We don't know how to compress molecules. It's still in the theory stage."

"Describe it as if it were fact."

"I don't know if I can. Theoretically you take, say, molecules of hydrogen and oxygen, squeeze them in a pressure unit and then freeze them to an inert state. Conceivably you could carry a swimming pool in a thimble. Use a little heat to release the molecules all at once, or slowly. There's so much work to be done in the field. It's only an idea. Who did you say was talking about it?"

"Supposedly some drunken derelict sent a message to Mr. Ennesto saying the Eldoron had used compressed molecules in the injections."

"Does Mr. Ennesto have the recorded message?"

"It was a written note and he threw it away. Why?"

"It seems to me that if the derelict knew what he was talking about he would have elaborated."

It seemed to Garly that nobody elaborated on anything nowadays. Unable to entreat or bully anyone into spelling out to him exactly what the tape in his body was and why it was there, he went off to make plans of his own. As long as the thing couldn't be gotten out of him he might as well learn to live with it. Besides, all the knowledgeable people with whom he had spoken assured him the tape was bound to have a limited life span. Any day now it would die and be cast off with the rest of his anatomical debris.

There was something he hadn't mentioned to the scientist. The derelict who supposedly knew all about the tapes had said that as long as the bearers stayed away from the Eldoron they would be safe. Garly didn't need anything else to convince him he ought to leave Olympus, not that he was positive his information was fact but it sounded better than anything else he had heard.

Cili had to go out of her apartment sometime, being a natural-born Olympian afflicted with a trace of claustrophobia. When she finally did the detectives Garly had hired picked her up.

It hadn't taken much planning. The jeep was serviced and ready to go, the small trailer was stocked with provisions and the way had been made clear for him by virtue of his political push and a volume of cash.

Nobody had ever told him how many ditches, gorges, streams and rocky inclines there were in the wilderness, nor had he any idea that a pair of centuries could grow such a tangle of trees and brush. For the first time in his life he regretted his slight stature.

Mostly he spent his time out of the jeep hacking a trail through green jungle with a machete, exhausting himself within minutes and then sitting on the front bumper to muse and talk to himself. Cili wouldn't help him, hadn't done much of anything but cry since he let her loose of the bonds with which the detectives had secured her. It somewhat bothered his conscience to look at her. She appeared about fourteen, all pink and white, pampered first by her mother and then by him. The thought came to him that she and Monkwell probably would have made a good duo. They both had the same kind of brain.

She tricked him, waited until he stopped and went well

ahead to hack out a trail, jumped out and headed back the other way at a startling clip. Luckily for him it was easier driving over a ready-made trail. It didn't take him long to overtake her but then he had to wait until she tired before he could get her into the jeep again. That took longer than he expected. At least her youth was good for something.

"We'll never get where we're going at this rate," he said as the machine rocked and pitched toward what looked like an impenetrable wall of weeds.

"Where are we going?" Cili wasn't crying now. She was too angry and tired.

Having no answer to her question he made no response, braked to a stop and dully stared at the work waiting for him.

She wouldn't get out to lend him a hand, hunkered in the jeep like an abused child and plotted to get away from him.

"You aren't going back," he said, hurling the machete to the ground and walking over to her. "Try to get that through your head. We're staying out here until Olympus' troubles are past."

"You had no right to kidnap me! What you did was illegal."

"That was back there in civilization. We left the law behind the moment we took the jeep out of that last tiled corridor."

Her shrewd little eyes never wavered. "You don't fool me. You only brought me along because you're afraid to be alone."

"That's possible. I'll confess the sight of you right now doesn't do much to me except make me irritable. Maybe you're my city girl. Whatever, it makes no difference."

"You can let me go. I'll follow the trail back."

'And leave me to face the frontier all by myself?" He returned to the green wall and put his failing energy to full use.

Toward evening he burst through the high weeds and found a broad valley stretched out ahead of him. There hadn't been many clear patches in the journey, so he was grateful to drive the jeep down a gentle incline and parked it just short of a wooded section.

Cili refused to help him pitch the tent, made herself as obnoxious as possible, probably hoped her presence would be too much for him and he would tell her to get out. The coming dusk wiped all such thoughts from his head.

Somewhere along the line the powers that led Olympus had

decided to do away with the nature bit and got rid of birds and all but essential insects. Consequently the city's night sounds were scarcely different from its day sounds. Out here in the wilds the coming night promised to be more terrifying than anything Garly had imagined. Who would have thought crickets were capable of creating such a din, and why had he never been told that birds made such a racket while settling down? He couldn't identify a third of the noises echoing through the valley.

"I didn't sleep a wink," Cili said in the morning.

Sitting up, Garly scratched his head. The sunlight breaking through the cracks around the tent flap surprised him. He'd been certain he wouldn't sleep at all. "What, you're still here?" he said.

"Did you think I'd take off in the dead of blackness? I stuck my head out once last night and that was enough. Not even the moon and the stars helped. All those old antique novels are a pack of lies, telling how hunters and trappers and lovers used the moon like we use flashlights. You can't see three feet in front of you out there after the sun goes down."

"How about some breakfast?"

"For myself. Do your own."

With a wry smile he said, "One thing I guessed rightly about you, you're no helpless little clinging vine. Think how you've deceived your poor mother."

The grim look on her face disappeared. "Let's both go back. Maybe people lived like this at one time, but the human personality changed over the centuries. We're no good for anything but easy living."

She took off shortly before noon while he was in the woods making a latrine. He was appalled to realized that he was alone in the valley with the weeds to his left, the monstrously high trees to his right and the unknown at his back. Her being there in the vicinity had helped hold in abeyance some of the terror.

It wasn't difficult to follow her since she made no secret about which way she went. No doubt she expected him to catch up with her and then take her on to Olympus. To prevent himself from being tempted to do such a thing, he followed her on foot, climbed out of the valley and located the chopped place where he had come out of the jungle the day before.

He liked it less and less as he traveled. Not that he couldn't find plenty of signs where she had passed, but the forest seemed to have grown over his trail in a single day and he found himself wandering in untouched territory. It was taking him too long to catch up with her.

He found where she had turned back. It was plain to read. Perspiring, chill with anxiety, he stood in brush that loomed over his head and tried to calm his speeding panic. Evidently she had decided to return to camp, for he was slow about overtaking her. But that wasn't the reason she had turned back, at least he didn't think so. Blinking sweat from his eyes, he studied the spittle on the leaves at hand height, the strands of long fur stuck in the wood of a tree stump, the crushed vines. So many crushed vines.

Something besides his wife had passed this way. That was why Cili turned back. Something was on her trail besides a man. Her pursuers were four-legged, about six of them.

It was a long while later that he lay in the brush at the top of the valley and stared down at the camp. Dusk cut off most of the light but he could still see how the tent sagged and flapped in the breeze. In fact, part of it had been ripped away. He was thinking that she had come back for the rifle, not knowing he had hidden it. When she decided to run away she couldn't sneak into the tent because he had been watching from the woods, so she took off empty handed. When she realized she was being followed by wolves she turned back to get the gun.

How hard she ran during those last few minutes. With the tent in sight, what had she hoped or thought as she flew across the ground? She could run like a deer and had gotten there ahead of them because they were cowardly and hung back until the last moment. She had burst into the tent with almost no breath left, having used her reserve to call out for help, though she hadn't really expected any help. In the tent, she grabbed for the rifle that had been hanging by the flap that morning.

Garly lay in the brush on the hill and whimpered. He was thinking of the dawn when he would have to go down and enter the tent. If only he hadn't stacked the food cartons inside. Then there would have been no need for him to go in.

Chapter XIII

Corradado lay blinking in the rain that fell on him from open skylights far over his head. He looked like an ancient stone statue, so still did he rest. The inhabitants of the city were numerous; there were always some at hand, to grasp and torment like a cat with a mouse.

Lethargy gripped him so that he didn't move out of range of the carnage of his own making but lay among mutilated corpses and allowed nature to take its course. Soon he would sleep. Instinctual buds in his brain were growing and would reach out into the environment to search for a suitable nest. The place where he slept must be hidden from prying eyes, must be somewhat unreachable. It would be best if no one could find him.

Rain pelted his head and made him look up. Probably the mechanisms that opened and closed the skylights needed repairing, a matter that had gone unattended to by shriekers more interested in saving their skins.

Water was four centimeters deep on the floors, had soaked into the upholstered furniture in the room which normally served as a museum. Now it was a temporary campground for the slayer from the sky. Abruptly changing his position, he lay down on top of a metal case the contents of which had been kicked onto the floor. The bones of human antiquity lay mixed with more contemporary ones.

Deep within the Fluger stirred a longing to enter the darkness of slumber. Another life period would begin after his rest. While sleeping he would gain weight and add more centimeters to his girth than he had done all year. His brain would develop more nodules of vitriol, which would enable him to bore through the hard mountains of Fluga, chase down plenty of swift and elusive rakka, stand up to challengers of his own kind, woo a maid and sire mighty children. It was too bad that his genes didn't know he needed to do none of those things anymore. Too bad for Olympus.

Rainwater leaked through ceilings and floors into a granary several levels below. The saturated grain swelled, rotted, stank. Engorged rats went scurrying.

The metal case creaked as Corradado rolled onto his back and let the rain wash his belly. On the homeworld he would have preferred a bath of lava. He wondered if the case would break under him. He hoped not because then he would lose sight of the cursed little shrieker squatting in a high el watching him.

Something in his brain moved and he relaxed. He could almost feel invisible sensors poking from his skull, probing the environment, seeking, reaching. There was warmth somewhere in the distance, not the kind that could be measured in degrees but the kind representing comfort and security.

Groaning, he rolled off the case, fell among the bones of long dead and newly dead shriekers. A skull with a rat in it stared into his yellow eyes. Again he he groaned, forced himself to crawl through the debris thrown at him by shriekers who hadn't been able to get out of the room. The archways had either collapsed or were blocked by furniture.

Like a sleepy cat, he plodded along until he reached the eastern wall, raised his paw and hit the partition a savage stroke, stood still while a large section fell in pieces on him. Though sleep was a drug that would eventually see him stiff and immobile, he was yet vicious enough to swipe his path clear and move into the boulevard.

The warmth drew him onward. Like the throbbing of a drum, it signaled its presence, seemed to promise a cessation of the pain of ennui seeping through his body. How difficult it was to tear holes in walls. Too often he couldn't be bothered to chase shriekers and kill them. Truly the warmth ahead was the thing he desired.

Like a dormant infection, hatred flared in him as he leaped onto a wall, ran up it like a huge insect and tried to tear away a moving el, just as the thing dipped away from him and sped in a horizontal direction toward the far end of the boulevard. Grimly he eyed it. The little shrieker in it was like the adult odd one. Crafty. But could he expect to stay forever beyond the reach of Corradado?

Angry, sulking, sleepy, he climbed down the wall and destroyed a section of the floor. Then he ran around the boulevard smashing things. Through one wall of the kitchen and out the other he went and then repeated his actions until the rounded walls fell down and the dispensers were exposed and ruined. Furniture was ripped to shreds and tossed about, bodies were clawed into strips and flung to the ceiling, intercom boxes were bitten off walls, archways were made impassable. Still the el rider moved overhead, alert, cautious, ever cunning.

The adjoining boulevard was on fire, had been burning for several hours. The extinguishers didn't work and the skylights were stuck and couldn't be opened to allow the rain to come in, not that the water would have dampened such an inferno, as the shriekers found out when the glass panels exploded. Corradado tore his way into the fire and paused in disappointment. Was this the warmth he had come so far to find? This was nothing but a tiny flame and wouldn't do at all.

As he stood staring at the dancing red and blue blossoms he reached outward with his mind and was immediately encouraged. It was still there. The warmth wasn't here at all. It was there farther on, beyond these puny licks of light.

One benefit of the fire was that it took the little shrieker off his trail, at least temporarily. Unlike himself, shriekers cringed from the least bit of flame, so he ran his last kilometer in absolute solitude. He was too close to the source, and the atoms of his strange blood were making him too rigid to worry about who might be following him.

There was no danger. There was no poison on Earth that could damage his internals, no missile in human existence that could pierce his unearthly flesh, no heat known to shriekers capable of burning him. It was simply the instinctual way. As far as his genes were concerned, he was still on Fluga, and must choose his sleeping nest wisely so that no psychotic Fluger found him. His instinct and his consciousness vied as he traversed shiny metal corridors toward the heart of Olympus. The beat of that heart told him he was heading in the right direction.

He entered a low archway beyond which lay a dim tunnel, paused to look back and considered that the little shrieker who had been following him for days might not have been dispatched by the fire. Conceivably the child had skirted the area and came around on his infernal els until the passage was clear and he could continue following.

Corradado placed a paw at the rounded edge of the archway overhead, shot out his claws, gripped and exerted gradual pressure. For the first time since he had come to this reality he was careful not to smash and rend.

Annoyed that the metal stretched only a bit, he applied more pressure. Still the metal failed to stretch. He created heat by raking his claws back and forth above the archway's edge and then quickly pulled on the same spot. The edge immediately lowered.

Applying heat to all sides of the opening, he pulled them together until not even a little shrieker could squeeze through. After that he continued on into shadowy places. It didn't occur to him that he was in a one-way corridor and that by sealing the way behind him he made his course obvious.

Section Five, Level One was the largest complex in Olympus. Built between the bottom of the fifth and sixth loops high above the ground, it was composed of tunnels, rooms, compartments, machines and the outlet at the top. Heavy and cumbersome, the complex was held up by mighty beams that ran nearly the entire length of the ten loops or O's where the millions lived and had their homes.

Far above the compartment toward which the Fluger headed was an area that looked like a nature scene with a small lake surrounded by sloping banks growing into tiers of rocks and brush. Here and there a tree jutted. Artificial atmosphere produced a sky of cumulus clouds floating against a blue backdrop with crooked light coming between the clouds like shattered beams. This was the outlet for the complex below.

The scenery was wasted since the area was closed to the public, and the few workmen who ventured there seldom took the time to appreciate the view. Regarding some matters, many people were old-fashioned or superstitious and the reactors beneath the water of the lake were enough to make mechanics and even technicians hurry through what they had to do. It was no good explaining to them how safe were the hearts of the city for imagination sent microscopic knives through protoplasm to slice and chop, to mutate genes, distort one's features and even deprive one of hair.

It didn't matter. The reactors would do their work for a thousand years. Practically all the maintenance they required could be done in the lower halls where the computers sat with watchful eyes that never closed.

Corradado prowled through dimly lit passages and approved of what he saw. He didn't hate the machines with their blinking lights nor did he wreak any destruction during his journey. The nest was just ahead and he was rapidly running out of energy. His blood continued to produce heavy particles that would nourish him during the coming days, while at the same time his brain swelled ever so slightly. Raising one paw after another became too torturesome for him; pushing his great weight through the light atmosphere was too burdensome.

Panic tried to light a spark within him by warning that he had waited too long to find a nest, but he paid it no heed. Instinct was his guardian now. A million years of struggling for survival had made Flugers independent except when they were the most vulnerable. Then their conscious minds dimmed and a more cunning and infallible monitor called the moves.

There were heat, darkness, power and danger to all but the creature in the tunnel above the squat machine, which was encased in a cage. Careful not to break anything, he climbed up a series of pipes, trying not to groan as he made the effort. He wasn't thinking normally now but listened to a voice no one else could ever hear since it issued directly from his subconscious. Sleep was not eternal but was merely a temporary cessation of vitriolic activity.

The tunnel above the squat machine was a perfect nest. As for the machine itself, it was snuggled within the security of heavy metal bulwarks that in no way inspired his admiration except in that the place was avoided by all shriekers. This he sensed. This was his security, provided him by the special nodules in his brain. Nothing on the planet presented the least menace for him save the shriekers who were worthy of nothing but contempt.

The pipes threatened to bend beneath his weight as he climbed, so he moved nearer to the reactor. Ten, twenty meters up he went, pausing now and then as the lead and other elements in his blood increased in density. He made the mistake of looking down and swayed with vertigo, had to grip the pipe with his claws but he did it with reserve so that the metal didn't collapse. Instinctively he knew that any damage done here would attract the attention of the shriekers.

At last then he was finished. Successfully he had accomplished it. Into the tunnel he poked his big head, smelled the smell of languor and solitude, placed his weight onto his front paws and hauled himself all the way in. By the time he had gathered the strength to crawl until he was directly above the reactor he was nearly done.

Memory stirred as he looked about. Where were the red rock walls of Fluga? Was he not deep within the mountains of home? All was well. No native of his homeworld would deliberately disturb him while he rested. It was the law. Grumpily he squirmed. There were too many laws. While he was still living with his parents he once asked his father why Flugers didn't drop all laws, forget they existed and have an all out war. Wasn't war what life was about? His father hadn't answered the question, but the young Fluger remembered how his eyes lit up at thoughts of such a battle.

Like a stone in fluid depths, his mind steadily and gently sank into a twilight that seemed infinite and permanent. Forgotten were all his plans for Flugers and shriekers. He didn't even care if this meant an eternal end for him.

His brain entered a condition of near calcification. So heavy was his blood that his body stiffened and became like petrified wood. His eyes closed, his vital signs plummeted on an imaginary scale to near zero. An entire year's wear and tear of the mortal coil was about to be attended to. Beneath him the squat structure hummed, perhaps in protest that its potential for savagery was also harnessed.

Corradado slept.

* * *

Addard was on his way home after having given a State of the Union message at a *tev* station. He hadn't made a good speech. Who could have, considering the situation? He was certain he hadn't inspired confidence in anyone.

The cabs couldn't be trusted anymore, so he rode in a four-wheeled, open, two-seated vehicle powered by a battery. There were two people in the car beside himself, the driver and a senator who kept assuring him that things would work out.

The senator's hands lay on his knees, pale white, or pink, or whatever that color happened to be. Addard had always looked for a perfect comparison. His own hands were near the senator's, several shades darker, brown and creased like cowhide.

He liked to tell himself that he had gone into politics for prestige and money, and perhaps those were legitimate reasons even for him, but they weren't primary. If he had been totally honest with himself he still couldn't have named that first motive.

On his twelfth birthday he became interested in genealogy, visited the microfiche unit in the library and began tracing his ancestry. What a shock it had been for him to discover he came from slaves. To be sure, he had learned of slavery in his history classes but that was something that happened centuries ago, antique and unreal or at least forgettable.

There was a photograph in the library stacks hidden inside an old twentieth-century volume. Addard hadn't been able to bring himself to destroy it. It was of a little old man dressed in rags, wizened and toothless, his hair like sheep's wool, grinning at whoever held the camera, a happy piece of property like a copying machine or a bed blanket. What succeeded in jarring Addard beyond repair was the fact that he could see a resemblance between himself and the old man. The slave.

For years he went about trying to notice whether or not white people treated him with contempt or at least condescension. It was the wrong thing to do and he realized it. There was no reading another mind and facial expressions and voice tones were private, subjective and defied interpretation.

He went into politics, made a name for himself and lived with a confident feeling in his viscera except on infrequent occasions when something happened to remind him of that old photograph.

Now the senator's voice droned on and on; the driver in the front seat manipulated the car through rooms, boulevards and corridors with facility while the mayor of Olympus sat brooding over a faded bit of knowledge.

The vehicle was only traveling a few kilometers an hour; when the front wheels hit a soft spot in the corridor and the machine suddenly dropped about a meter as the floor gave way, no one was hurt. Stunned but not injured. There were so many citizens helping them out of the hole that the situation took on humorous overtones. Laughing, joking, the three were lifted onto solid flooring.

Hands dusted Addard's back and shoulders. a voice assured him that another car waited just through a nearby archway and if he would only come this way, just around the corner. . . .

As he entered the opening two things occurred to him. The room was quite dark and the voice sounded familiar. At about that time something made of cloth dropped over his head, enveloped his shoulders, captured his arms so tightly he couldn't move them.

He opened his mouth to yell but lost his breath as someone grabbed him and flew with him into the air. All of a sudden he was too terrified to do anything but cringe. The higher they went the sicker he became until he moaned with the effort of keeping his mouth clamped shut.

It took a long time to arrive at their destination. In between flying bouts Kam Shar stood on unsteady perches, inched along narrow pathways, crouched in hiding or simply walked with his burden clasped in his arms.

Addard recognized the place as soon as he succeeded in working the straitjacket up over his head. The strings had been left untied, otherwise he never would have made it. Now he glanced up in time to see the winged man step onto an open el and glide upward through a fluffy white cloud.

"Come back!" Addard called. He threw away the jacket and looked around, first with curiosity and then in alarm. The knowledge that he stood on top of nuclear reactors filled him with consternation.

There was no need for him to be disturbed for he knew perfectly well where the exits were, having given this area more than one official and unnecessary inspection.

It turned out, however, that he had reason to be nervous. The northern exit panel was closed across the archway and no amount of approaching it in the proper manner would cause it to slide back. The same was true of the eastern archway. Perplexed, exhausted, he began walking along the lake toward the southern exit.

Hours later he lay beneath an apple tree on one of the tiers of sod and listened to the beating of his heart. The day of reckoning seemed to have arrived. Kam Shar had brought him here to the park and here he would stay until someone came to let him out. There was fruit to eat and warm water to drink, if he didn't mind using the stuff that cooled the reactors deep beneath him. It was clean and uncontaminated, so he had been told. He didn't believe it, though. Not that it mattered. Food and drink were unimportant to him now. The proud son of slaves was taken prisoner by a white man. Again.

Turning onto his back, he snorted. If he couldn't be courageous the very least he could be was rational.

The city planners had kept reality in mind; at eight-thirty in the evening the crooked light coming into the park was cut off. Addard had a few stars and a slight breeze to keep him company. Other than that he was alone. Not even the hum of the buried hearts reached his level.

He didn't sleep, didn't even try to. His life hung in the balance, he knew, but more important the life of Olympus was at stake, and he had always possessed a fierce love for his birthplace. How fortunate he was to have been born in a city where there were all the physical comforts, where a good education was available and a significant career was ready for him to pursue.

His body relaxed. Black or white, mayor or dreg, they would make an accounting, each citizen in the city and most especially all those whom Kam Shar brought here to the park. There were bound to be others. The park was going to be the arena. Addard and all those who had been injected with the tapes were the gladiators.

It didn't help even after Monkwell came. Certain that he wouldn't doze, Addard awakened from deep sleep, sat up and looked into the frozen visage of his adviser. The red-haired man's freckles stood out against the pallor of his face as he sat on his heels watching and waiting.

They retraced Addard's steps of the evening before in an effort to find a way out. All the archways were securely closed. Monkwell knew where there was an intercom in a steel box buried to the lid in one of the tiers of sod. They found it but it didn't function, had probably been disconnected underground. A metal column running from floor to ceiling near the lake served as a maintenance shack for the area, containing tools and several intercoms but the doors were locked. Several *tev* cameras were built into trees fringing the lake and they went from one to another hoping they were operating, hoping someone would see and come to investigate.

Monkwell had been brought there at gunpoint by Kam Shar.

"He was wearing his human suit," he said bitterly. "No explanations, no greeting, no nothing."

"I expect to lose the next election," said Addard.

"This is a swell time to make jokes."

"It was no joke."

"We'll be lucky to have an election. A combination of rain, acid, fire and just plain destruction have done an expert job on the shafts between Sections Two and Three."

"They won't fall."

Frowning, Monkwell said, "We'd better hope they don't. Just imagine it. The ceilings and all the walls sag and create extra weight on the floor which has been half eaten away. Suddenly it breaks. All at once there's an empty space between loops where the part fell out. Nothing to hold up the western column, nothing to stabilize all the other loops and the eastern column. And her fall was a mighty one, full of blood and thunder."

"They'll fix it. They're working on it right now. I know they are."

They finally gave up trying to get out. The exits were sealed, the intercoms were dead, the ceiling els wouldn't come down no matter how vigorously they pressed the buttons on the wall panels. Monkwell didn't know where Kam Shar had gone and didn't care.

"He put me in a ceiling el, rode down with me and made me get out. Then he went back up. He must have rewired the circuit so that he could have full control inside the machine."

"But there's more than one. They're all across the ceiling."

"Only one works. We should have shot him the first time he showed his face."

"Which one?" said Addard.

Chapter XIV

While Quantro Tilzer was hurrying away from the jewelry store in the city of Superior and losing himself in one of the many cab stations on the boulevard, the broadcasting booth on the corner blared away: "To all roving units, burglar is white-complected, seventy-two years of age, white-haired, white of beard, one-seventy-five centimeters tall, seventy-five kilos in weight, dressed in blue slacks and shirt. . . ."

The machine didn't leave much to the imagination, having received its information from a computer in the store, which had assessed data taken from cameras and scanning grids in front of or upon which Quantro had walked. The theft hadn't been difficult but neither had it been as covert as he might have wished. The jeweler had brought out the case of sparklers and then obeyed the robber's instructions to sit down and wait five minutes before notifying the police.

There had been the matter of funds. Life in Superior was every bit as expensive as in Olympus and he couldn't very well try the subsistence people without being asked how he had gotten into the city. He had already tried to enter the section where refugees from Olympus came in hourly, but police cordons sealed off all entrances and exits. It appeared that the mayor of Superior intended to keep Olympians isolated, perhaps in preparation for sending them back home should the opportunity present itself.

It also appeared that Wendelar didn't appreciate thieves, since several police officers were making inquiries at the apartments in Bachelor Row where Quantro had been living. Cursing his bad luck, he left that area and went to a section where it rained most of the time. People couldn't very well take a good look at him and recognize him as the jewel thief if they were protecting their own faces. However, while that might be to his advantage, it wasn't pleasant to sit soaking wet at tables in kitchens wondering what was to become of him.

He walked into a clothing store with the idea of buying at least an umbrella but the proprietor stared at him so pointedly that he left before his turn came to be waited upon. Tramping along grilled walkways. listening to the rain as it washed into troughs beneath his feet, he toyed with the idea of forcing his way into someone's apartment.

By midnight he still hadn't done it, hadn't found a place to stay other than a park bench. The temperature was constant and comfortable and in spite of his planning he fell asleep. It had been a long and arduous day and he was no longer youthful. That was where they found him the next morning, the jewels in his pocket.

Perhaps he subconsciously willed himself to be apprehended. In retrospect he thought he might have. As he lay on a soft bed in a comfortable cell he wondered if his zest for living had been conquered by adversity. No matter, he would get it back with a little easy living.

It wasn't but a few hours before they came to transfer him. He was a model prisoner, obeying every suggestion made by his guards. moving with alacrity, answering every question honestly and without hesitation. The fact that his cooperative attitude didn't help him made him even angrier than he would have been had he played dead and forced them to drag him.

"I know for a surety that this is illegal," he said. This time he did play dead but they didn't care, picked him up and handcuffed him into one of the plane's passenger seats. They weren't going to keep him incarcerated at all, didn't plan to give him the usual battery of psychological tests and they certainly weren't going to spend another dime of tax money on him once they dumped him back in Olympus where he belonged.

"But I don't want to go!" he said to the guards who stood on each side of him. "Haven't you heard my plea for amnesty?"

"Doesn't matter," one of the guards said. "We stopped accepting Olympians right after your Fluger began his fun and games. Now we're taking in a fixed quota."

"Can't I be included as a refugee?"

"You would, normally, but Wendelar says they want you back."

Quantro struggled against the handcuffs that kept his wrists locked to the chair arms. "That's crazy! I'm as worthless over there as I am here or anywhere."

"I believe you. They tell me your other alien, the one from Eldoron, requested extradition in your case, and I hear that bird gets just about whatever he asks for."

"I'm done, then!" Quantro slumped in the seat. "It's over. I don't have a chance."

"All that's over are your pilfering days in a city that doesn't want you. Cheer up, old buddy. You might beat the odds."

There was no cheer in him as he watched the plane hurry down the runway and take off. The doors closed and he was left alone in a private hangar of bright crooked light and too many echoes. He was back in Olympus. He was home again.

"You had no right!" he called into the emptiness around him. Was that someone moving up there near the ceiling? He stopped, squinted, saw that he had been mistaken. The els were motionless and unoccupied. "Why did you pick me?" he said in a loud voice. "I'm not responsible for anyone's duties but my own. You're an alien, what we humans consider a dangerous animal. Who do you think you are coming in here and dropping your gavel on me? Why should I be a sacrifice for somebody else?"

He continued walking because to stop meant surrendering to the case of nerves that made his knees knock and his neck itch. Somehow he had lost his facility for utilizing oxygen. The air seemed thick and black-specked.

An ebony colored animal came through the archway at the far end of the hangar. The sight of it disturbed Quantro but he was more concerned with his chest. Every time he breathed

143

his throat made squeaking sounds. The air went down like a dozen knives that entered his bosom and severed vital connections.

"Don't you ever change your mind?" he asked. "Never a lapse of memory? Can't you forget about me, let me go back to being what I've always been?"

He was breathing better by the time the black beast stopped beside him. As he straddled the broad back the only sign of his distress was in the thin tears trickling down his cheeks.

Garly sat on the hill above the campsite with the collar of his jacket turned up to protect his neck. He hadn't consciously pulled it up, just as he hadn't consciously done much of anything for many days. Sometimes he wandered away to pick berries or gnaw at the bark on trees but usually he could be found sitting or lying on the hill with his dead eyes fastened on the tent.

"You'll go down, won't you?" was the first thing he said to the winged man who flew down out of nowhere.

Kam Shar looked at him closely. "What?"

"I've been waiting for you. Or someone. To go down."

The alien's eyes followed the pointing finger. Stepping to the edge of the incline he made a diving motion and then stilled in a horizontal position for an instant or two as his wings extended and gathered air. He flew out over the valley and descended to the tent.

Garly was gnawing a piece of bark when he returned. Elevating his wings into high arrows, the Eldoron sat beside him.

"You've lost a great deal of weight."

"Have I?" Garly didn't make mention of anything Kam Shar might have seen below. "I don't have much appetite."

"You look to be in very poor health."

The other shrugged.

"I buried what was left of the body."

Tears spilled from the adviser's eyes. "Body? What body?"

"How long have you been out here?"

"I don't know."

"Don't eat that. It will make you sick."

"There isn't anything else."

144

Kam Shar held out a hand. "Come along. I'll take you back to the city. But you won't be competing with the others. I'm eliminating you."

Garly's madness fell away from him for at least those few moments. "You're talking about the tape inside me and the Fluger. I won't be eliminated, do you understand?"

"She has nothing to do with the Fluger."

"Oh, yes, she does. She had everything to do with it. I brought her out here because I wanted company while I was saving my skin. Then I didn't even have the decency to go down and help her. Every night I listen to their howls as they run in after her, every time I fall asleep I see them drag her down. You see, I got back here before they did. I guess I took a shortcut or something. Maybe I could have killed them all with my gun. She didn't have anything. Did you ever hear someone scream while being torn to pieces?"

"Every day since I've been on this planet. You're deranged. You can't compete."

"I can. I long for it."

"It wouldn't be just."

"In my opinion it will," said Garly, thinking that now he wouldn't have to shoot himself.

Ennesto lay in his bed with the sheet drawn up to his chin and listened to the popping sound of pistols. Like corks bursting from champagne bottles the sounds continued in the living room as his guards warded off some unidentified invader.

Of course the invader wasn't unknown. The old man was well aware of who was trying to get into the apartment after him. Had it been the Fluger the guards would either have killed it or deserted their posts. Any ordinary citizen would be dead by now and the firing would have stopped. It hadn't, so naturally it had to be the alien again, playing another one of his games as he attempted to reach the bedroom.

"You don't fool me!" he shouted. "I know you can get in here in a second. You're trying to prep me for a trip somewhere but it doesn't matter how long you play because I won't be ready. I'm not going anywhere!"

The head guard came in to report that the front entrance

panel refused to stay closed but kept sliding back and forth as if it were off its runner.

"It probably is!" yelled Ennesto. "Fix it!"

But if they did that, the guard explained, they would have to put down their guns and then the man in the corridor could walk right in.

The harassment had been going on all morning. "Leave me alone!" Ennesto whined to his unseen foe. "Can't you see I'm old? You can't possibly need me for anything. All I'm good for is intellectual labor."

The *tev* over his bed clicked on and to his astonishment the image of Kam Shar appeared on the screen. He was a man this morning, similar to a human but not exactly the same. He was too slender and his hair was too wavy but the eyes were the real clue that brought to mind visions of unearthly climes.

"Good morning, Adviser," said Kam Shar. "You're correct in assuming that I'm prepping you for a journey which will be brief. I do this instead of simply marching into your domicile and claiming you, because you require special attention."

"And because my men will blow you to kingdom come."

"Did you ever hear of a firing jammer?"

The longer he talked the more nervous Ennesto became. The alien couldn't possibly be communicating through the *tev*, no matter if he appeared to be doing just that. "Don't give me any double baloney," he said.

"You've never heard of a firing jammer? Pay attention and you will."

Ennesto waited for something to happen. Meanwhile, it dawned on him that he couldn't hear corks popping. "Get off my screen!" he howled. "Get away from my house! I don't care how many fancy machines you brought with you. Maybe the guns won't work but what can you do to stop knives and blackjacks? Answer me that, mister!"

"Freeze them. A little care directing the signal . . . you see, it has a light-metal detector. . . ."

Ennesto bellowed for the head guard.

"We might as well quit," he said, coming into the bedroom. "Nothing works."

"You do," said the old man, "and you'd better continue or I'll fire you and your whole crew."

146

"That wouldn't hurt our feelings."

"I'll see to it that you never work again!"

"Why don't you try showing a little gratitude? We're staying because we don't want anyone dragging you from your bed. There's no need for threats."

Nothing did any good. The metal weapons brandished by the guards literally broke in pieces, the guns wouldn't fire, the blackjacks crumbled, brass knuckles grew rings of light around them and frightened their wearers, who couldn't seem to get them off quickly enough.

The front entrance panel suddenly slid aside and the guards rushed through it to take the alien in their hands, but he moved like fast smoke out of their reach. Before they knew it he was inside the apartment while they were locked out. A few minutes later, when he emerged with Ennesto in a wheelchair, a little puff of gas preceded him. The guards fell over in various states of unconsciousness and the alien and his prisoner moved out of range to an unknown destination.

He didn't enjoy doing it but he didn't tell them that. Either they knew it already or they considered him a butcher. What did it matter what they thought? It wouldn't change anything.

It was the same everywhere, bewildered men of consequence waiting for fate to send them a miracle that would rid them of the menace threatening their world. A Fluger or one of the other murderers inhabiting the planets that spun around suns—men always faced them in the same manner, irrationally and ineffectually.

He had seen them all, not literally, but the hordes of death-dealers were there in his memory, sometimes faceless and at other times no more than a wisp of thought, all savage and lawless, all plundering worlds peopled with men such as the four who stood gray-faced and rigid while they listened to his words.

There was no other way and he trusted that they realized as much. If the Fluger wasn't stopped after this sleep period there wouldn't be another chance for an entire year, by which time Kappa would be gone. Make no mistake, there was no weapon here that could bring down a young Fluger. The Kappans were only fortunate in that they hadn't shipped on an adult specimen.

As the leaders of the city of Olympus the four were naturally willing and prepared to make the sacrifice that would destroy the enemy. It was always done this way; never in his experience had the Eldoron known a people to turn their faces from him at the final moment. No, not once. This was his work and he did it well.

He wanted to impress upon them that the Fluger was growing while asleep and that when he awakened he would be much more vicious than before. It would require only a matter of weeks before he brought the city tumbling down, literally made it into a twisted, smoking mound of trash that would litter the landscape for a thousand centuries. Being intelligent, the Fluger would proceed to look for more Kappans. He would find the other cities. One by one he would destroy them. In a matter of months there would be no more world, no more people or cities. Nothing. Not even the slum towns would be left untouched by the killer whose nature and joy it was to prowl and raze.

So then the four and Kam Shar would kill him. How? Inside their bodies, and this included the other two bodies belonging to the Eldoron, were tapes bearing a great many compressed molecules of a special substance. After the Fluger ate one of the tapes he would die.

Hulian didn't know if any of the weapons would be effective, but he placed them in the bag one by one, all the instruments of mayhem he had accrued over the days and weeks. Large and small, they went into the bag along with ammunition. When he had them all packed he prepared to leave.

"You're a little fool!" said Roxey and tried to grab him, but Hulian was quick and agile and made it outside. From there it was a matter of running faster, unlatching els and boarding more rapidly, locating cabs, things Roxey could do with efficiency but not as well as a sighted person.

After he knew he had lost the boy, the man went down into the levels where the hearts pumped, tramped up and down corridors searching for an unbarricaded pipe or shaft leading up to the reactors' outlet. Everyone in the city and probably in the world knew where they were, having been gifted with elaborate explanations on the *tev* by Kam Shar. He must have a liver like a chunk of steel to be able to say such things without moving a hair. Speaking softly and telling about those five poor saps locked up like a bunch of turkeys waiting for the ax to fall. Naturally Kam Shar hadn't mentioned the boy, otherwise someone might have objected and then a mob would have taken down every exit in the park no matter how tightly they were sealed. At least Roxey hoped someone would be concerned about Hulian, someone besides himself.

The boy had a one-track mind; maybe the Eldoron couldn't be expected to understand fully the human personality, but he should have checked the loose ends before letting the youngster handle the cameras. There the picture was on the screen, which meant he was in that top el doing his job. Roxey knew this because everyone around him in the boulevard was describing what he saw. There were the mayor and his three advisers wandering through the park as if they had ghosts on their trail, and didn't they wish that was all it was? Let the whole city see what was happening. Why? Why not? Wasn't it their world?

There was Kam Shar, with wings, standing on the top tier in the center of the park, not watching the lake but looking everywhere, first right then left, his eyes never pausing but continually darting in all directions.

The boy, what was he doing? Roxey asked the question a dozen times and a dozen times he was told that there was no boy in the park. It was just the blind man's opinion that there was someone in the ceiling el and besides what could anyone do about it now?

Roxey ran and climbed, rode els and cabs until at last he stood beside the eastern entrance to the upper complex. He pounded on the archway until his fists were discolored with bruises. Eventually he sank down and leaned his head against the panel.

Addard and Monkwell stood at the eastern edge of the lake, where the tiers were interrupted and a small passageway began that led to the arched exit. After a while Monkwell edged away. He didn't say anything, just gave Addard a closed look and then went up onto the nearest tier. Addard couldn't blame him. Why pick somebody to keep company when you might very well end up dying with him?

He grew uneasy standing there in the narrow causeway, where the growing tiers on each side of him seemed to hang over him like walls of falling earth. Emulating Monkwell, he climbed onto the nearest tier and walked up the scaled levels until he was at the top.

Built like a stadium, the place suddenly seemed too small for him. He looked at the lake, envisioned the Fluger coming up out of it like a vengeful Neptune. It was too near. He backed up, felt the wall, was forced to stop. There was nowhere to go except up, but the els were unreachable. There was nowhere to go.

A haphazard bone—pick up a sap off the street, inject him with the tape and toss him in front of the Fluger. No.

Inject an animal and throw it into the deadly jaws of the yellow one, but the Fluger had chosen his preferred food weeks ago and would eat nothing else.

Gas him, chop, rend, mash, blow to hell, kill, kill, kill. Sorry, only the tape would work. The signal? The knowledge of impending death. Like a rapier the thought flashed through the brain and just as quickly the radiant energy triggered the minuscule battery in the tape, releasing the compressed molecules. That was how it would happen.

Kill, kill, with the savagery of hatred and desire. But it was no good. No man had that kind of brain power. Not even Mr. Know-It-All from the sky. He was in it with them to the end. Would he try to sneak away at the last moment? After all, he had wings and four legs. Two more pairs. Eight in all. The advantage was there.

Addard wondered how his heart could tolerate the things that were happening inside him. He looked up and experienced an overwhelming longing to see the real sky. If he died inside this artificial world—if the Fluger ate him—his molecules would never mix with his home sod. Somehow the thought depressed him. What possible difference could it make where he died? He couldn't answer his own question but his depression persisted, grew more intense, threatened to suffocate his fear.

Chapter XV

────────

Hulian trained the number-three camera on the center of the lake, where, in his opinion, the Fluger would make his entrance. According to Kam Shar the creature could come out anywhere in the complex, conceivably even outside it, but Hulian chose the lake.

He hadn't followed the killer into the lower tunnels leading to the reactors. It wasn't necessary. After he reported the sealed archway to Kam Shar, the alien took him to the park outlet and showed him all the metal shafts leading deep into the city. The Eldoron climbed down one of them after having donned a thin, mesh suit.

Through pipes and tunnels he crawled until he was directly above the sleeping animal where he fastened a device onto the metal wall. It would lead the Fluger in an upward direction. Containing an electronic heart, it was even now sending an invisible probe into the sleeping creature, reading pressures and temperatures.

Corradado's readings would change when he awakened. On his own world there would be peace and silence when his sleep was finished, not that a tranquil environment ever served to make a Fluger's reentry into his upper home a quieter one. However, when he came to wakefulness this time the device in the shaft above him would know it because of the changes in his body. It would begin broadcasting raucous sound, an ear-splitting explosion of noise calculated to dictate the direction of his furious exit. He would hate the noise and try to find its source. It wouldn't really have one since it merely

151

pitched signals northward and faded after a few minutes. By then he should be up in the arena where he was supposed to die.

In full view of the populace of Olympus the Fluger was supposed to expire. Kam Shar wasn't one to leave important incidents to occur in secrecy. Hulian understood this. Any number of things could happen or go wrong and the alien wanted the city kept abreast of every event; in case there was no one left alive in the complex to tell them.

The loud noise would infuriate the already maniacal Fluger who would try to catch it and rip it apart. Since the sound would remain above him, he would climb. He probably wouldn't destroy the reactor and the corridors around it because he would be boring upward through tunnels and shafts after the fading noise. By then his course would be set and he would be too angry to change his mind. Also, he would be ravenously hungry. He would remember that there were always people in the upper levels.

The cameras trained on the ground scene, Hulian crouched in the el which was now situated just below the clouds. He considered that he had failed his first test as a son. He loved Roxey but had disobeyed him; as he had the old man in the slum town; always running in the wrong direction, loafing when he ought to have been working, laughing at serious moments, not even there when the old soul needed him for the last time.

He saw Addard look up at him, saw the mayor wave to him. The old guy with the white beard, the one called Quantro, hadn't moved a centimeter since Kam Shar in four-legged form had walked in and deposited him beside the lake. He was on his knees staring at the water.

Better move, old man, Hulian thought. *Better move.*

The one called Garly had to be out of his mind, sat on his heels on the second tier northward glaring up at nothing. Once in a while he picked up a handful of dirt and sifted it through his fingers, but mostly he sat and looked skyward.

Ennesto was on the move searching for a way out, examining the manhole covers to see if any had loosened, trying the sealed archways, running his hands over the western wall, seeking, hunting for an escape route.

Monkwell was in a tree on the highest tier by the south wall. Sitting on a branch near the top, he didn't move, never stirred, just sat with his gaze fastened on the lake.

Kam Shar sat on the fourth tier southward near the eastern wall. His wings in repose behind him, he looked like a statue, so still did he rest. Incredibly, he slowly turned and lay on his stomach, stretched to full length and closed his eyes.

Addard had been watching him and appeared agitated by what he saw, began pacing back and forth along his tier, stepping now and then to the edge as if he intended to leave his position. Perhaps he didn't think his executioner should sleep at a time like this. Perhaps he realized he too would eventually have to lie down and close his eyes.

In a hangar at the airport a spaceship sat waiting for Kam Shar. If he survived, it would take him away from the world of Earthlings or Kappans. His tools, clothes and weapons were stored in a box, there for him to own and make use of if he lived. Two cartons lay open and ready to receive his alter forms.

Roxey stayed outside the eastern archway of the park complex, sleeping when he was exhausted, eating when he couldn't ignore his stomach, going away from the wall long enough to visit a washroom. He wanted Hulian to live. Now and then he glanced at the *tev* on the wall over his head and just as frequently he wished the machines weren't everywhere. He couldn't see the images there but he could imagine them and he wished he would stop. He had already lost one son.

Cili's mother stayed in front of her *tev* every waking hour. She hated the time wasted in sleep. She might miss it if she didn't keep her eyes open. She wanted Garly to come out of the park in one piece so she could ask him why her daughter hadn't come home. He would know. He had to.

Monkwell's wife couldn't bear to watch the *tev* but neither could she bear not to know. She kept her radio on low. Wherever she went in the apartment she kept one ear tuned to the announcer's voice: "Nothing has happened yet. Nothing yet. They're still waiting. And while they're waiting we're hoping that at least one of them dies. Has there ever been such an occasion in the history of this planet that we should desire the death of an individual so that the rest of us might live?"

No one waited for Addard or Ennesto. The one was a loner while the other had outlived his friends.

Two people watched for Quantro Tilzer but he never once thought of them. His concentration was upon his viscera. For a drink he would have given an arm. He didn't need his arms for running. For a full bottle he would have sold his soul. It would be a cheap trade.

They heard him long before they saw him. It began as a low rumbling sound that made the ground seem to move everywhere in the park. Monkwell cried out. The others appeared to be frozen in their tracks. More likely they were considering which way to run, while realizing any movement at all might jeopardize them even more.

The trees swayed as the earth shook. The lake swelled and created a tide that began hitting the shore with heavy blows. Here and there a tier split or collapsed. It was impossible for those in the park to tell where Corradado would emerge. They only knew he was coming.

Up out of the second tier north came the clawing, spitting behemoth in an enormous fountain of spewing sod that hadn't settled to the ground by the time he reached for his first victim.

Garly never knew what hit him; in fact was in the act of turning around to face his fate when the big paw came from nowhere and literally knocked his head off. He had calculated the odds and decided he would have to use the gun on himself after all. He didn't mind the thought of dying; anything to end his dreams. Since his luck was generally bad it would continue to be so and he would survive this outrageous battle. The Fluger might kill everyone else but it wouldn't kill him. He reached inside his shirt to feel for the gun and at the same moment he turned to watch while the yellow demon came and wiped out his companions. The ground pitched and swayed beneath his feet and the noise of splitting metal and breaking sod behind him was deafening. His last thought was that he was going to fall. That was when he felt the quick pain at the back of his neck.

Corradado savagely threw the corpse onto its back, stripped away the cloth and outer flesh and fed.

Ennesto had been too close to the point of entry, otherwise he might have made it away, at least for the time being. In spite of himself he cast a glance backward as he ran and saw what looked like a bubbling, scarlet splotch inside torn shirt and pants. The realization that this was Garly sent him into shock. He forgot who and where he was and simply ran as fleetly as he could, which was too fast for his worn heart. Up the tiers he staggered, apparently changed his mind and raced back down toward the lake to run along the water's edge. About midway he collapsed.

His movements had attracted the attention of the Fluger who was nosing through Garly's empty clothes. With three or four long bounds the yellow killer was upon his second victim. Neither had known he was about to die. Neither had had the time to trigger the tape inside his body.

Kam Shar flew upward to an el above the clouds, came back into view a moment later with his black animal body in his arms. Laying it on the ground, he fell down beside it. In an instant he transferred his life force from the winged form into the other. The black beast sprang to its feet and ran toward Corradado who was ripping at the corpse of Ennesto. It leaped across the Fluger's back, raking him with its claws as it went. It appeared to the onlookers that he would make it free and clear, but in a flash the Fluger whirled and caught him between two paws.

No sooner had he caught it than the black beast went limp. Kam Shar's spirit had fled. Corradado didn't eat the beast but began tearing it apart. The winged man who lay on the ground sat up and started screaming as if in agony. Seemingly in great pain, he staggered erect and stood watching as the furry body that was a part of his soul was savagely dismembered.

Corradado seemed enraged at the sight of Monkwell sitting on a top branch of a tree. Its foliage was too sparse to conceal him. While the red-haired man watched and waited for the murderer to reach him, an el came down from the ceiling and a small figure in it fired an arrow with accuracy. It went straight into the Fluger's gaping mouth.

With a cry of anger Corradado stopped to pluck out the

155

offending dart. Then without warning he made what might have been the best leap of his life straight up at the wobbling machine. He never reached it. Instead his arms were filled with the winged man from Eldoron who flew between him and the el holding Hulian. From under a shallow layer of dirt near the western end of the complex came a piercing scream and then Kam Shar in human form climbed out of his temporary grave in time to be witness to the extinction of another part of himself.

Corradado possessed an almost insatiable appetite and was eager to sample the flesh of the odd one who had tormented and piqued him for so long a time. Wings or no this body fit his requirements for a meal, so it was with zest that he consumed the corpse. He had no way of knowing that Kam Shar had accepted his own death before fleeing the doomed form. The knowledge of at least partial extinction was sufficient for the mindless mechanism in the tape. The process was triggered. The end began.

The el climbed higher as Hulian shot and threw missiles at the gluttonous Fluger. Then he went on up to the ceiling and accomplished another part of his task. The Eldoron had signaled him to press the button releasing all the exits.

Kam Shar stood on the fourth tier in the center of the park north and shouted. "It is done! The sacrifice is over! Save yourselves! The exits are open!" Again and again he shouted it, trying to attract the attention of those who still lived.

Addard tried to run but couldn't. Horrified by the deaths, benumbed by their violence, he stood with tears on his face and threw rocks at the Fluger. He couldn't run and he had no weapon but he couldn't bring himself to flee to safety while the remains of human and inhuman bodies lay all around him. Somehow he had to avenge all those wounds, so he threw rocks and wept.

Quantro Tilzer and Monkwell stared from the distant figure of the Eldoron to the exits.

"We have succeeded!" he cried. "Save yourselves! Run! Get out!"

How long did he have? The question burned feverishly in Quantro's brain. There was the eastern exit and there was the western one. Why had he placed himself halfway? He had a

156

couple of minutes to stay clear of the Fluger. That's what Kam Shar had told them. A couple of minutes after he ate a knowing victim. Eating Garly hadn't counted, since Garly hadn't been aware of his impending death. Ennesto hadn't known either, but then the Fluger hadn't even eaten all of him.

A couple of minutes, and Quantro didn't know that behind his back Corradado was choosing between him and the shrieker in the tree, didn't know how vividly the Fluger remembered the hated smell of whisky and a high mound of junk behind a little apartment. Even more than the Eldoron, Corradado desired to feel in his jaws the shrieker with the foul stink who had caused him trouble.

Was that the sound of running feet behind him? Quantro groaned, ran as fast as he could toward the eastern exit. It was open! He could see through it and there were people everywhere. They were looking at him and they were screaming and trying to climb over one another to get back out of the way.

He staggered, tripped and fell, turned onto his back. "I'm sorry!" he cried. "I'm truly sorry! I didn't mean any of it!"

The Fluger spread itself on top of him, took his head in its teeth, bit in. Suddenly the creature paused. Reality suddenly seemed to move in slow motion for him. There was a hot sensation in his belly.

Actually, it was packing compound, the kind that swelled and hardened when wet. The full feeling had begun after he ate the winged man. Perhaps he shouldn't have dined on something unlike the average shrieker. No matter, he had all his strength or certainly enough to sample the guts of this stinking old one who had brought some misery into his existence. And so he did.

He ought to have been still hungry enough to eat all of the bearded one but for some reason he felt as if he had already eaten two dozen. Belching, he looked behind him and there was the little shrieker aiming a gun at his eye. The boy fired and hit him squarely on the eyeball with a little lead pellet that slid to the side of the white part and then went around and around the eye a few times before finally ricocheting away.

With a growl he lunged at the little one. The tape in his stomach released more and more compressed molecules.

157

Warmed by his internal heat they opened, mixed with his gastric juices, swelled and swelled.

Hulian turned and raced away. He dropped the gun and the bow and arrow and reached out for the el. Instead of grabbing hold of it he accidentally hit it a hard blow that made it swing upward to a height of about three meters. Now he couldn't reach it at all.

Kam Shar was suddenly there beside him. "Run," he said. "Hurry. He's still strong."

"Why should I? You already gave two parts of yourself."

The Fluger was coming at them like a clumsy elephant. H seemed middle heavy. Now and then he fell flat onto his stomach. With a dismayed expression on his face he fell again, reached out to ensnare both shriekers, found they had both fled.

Roxey had come into the complex as soon as the panels opened. Now he leaped again and again until he snagged the bottom of the el, hauled it down and held it while the Eldoron lifted Hulian into it.

"No!" yelled the boy as the machine moved upward.

"And stay there!" Roxey yelled at him.

Rolling onto his back Corradado gave a scream of rage. How much he longed to give chase. How heartily he desired to slay and rend for as long as time lasted. There was still a great deal on this planet to hold the interest of a young Fluger, so why did he lie here like a dead rakka doing nothing?

He lumbered to his feet, tore up a little bit of turf, stumbled forward and broke into a halting run that ate up the ground between him and the two men. They ran away from the eastern exit, climbed tiers until they reached the north wall. Hulian dropped a camera on him.

Corradado stopped to consider what was happening inside him. He didn't know that in his belly he had enough packing compound to fill ten bathtubs. Like flower buds the compressed molecules warmed and grew to normal size. The particles of compound absorbed stomach juices, drew upon the fluid in adjoining organs, swelled and began soaking up the contents of the thick blood vessels. The load in the stomach grew and created pressure, shoved things out of the way, increased and increased and didn't stop increasing.

He placed one paw on the tier and looked up at the shriekers through bloodshot eyes. A wad of something hard was embedded deep in his throat. He tried to cough it out as he advanced up the incline.

A few people came back to the open archways. One or two ventured into the park. They were silent. The loudest sound was the hacking of the Fluger as he attempted to rid himself of his deadly meal.

Monkwell climbed from the tree and slowly walked across the beach. Corradado turned his head to look at him. The hard wad in his throat was also deep inside him, shoving against his tender parts, threatening to break through his bowel. The sides of his stomach were splitting. His intestines had accepted the soft white powder which was expanding and hardening as it took up all the moisture in its vicinity.

It wasn't easy to kill a Fluger. This one had a tough heart which was well protected high up in his chest. The white material seemed purposefully to go after the throbbing organ, surrounded it, sucked it and packed it tightly. In spite of the pressure it continued its task.

Dull of spirit, Corradado glared at those whom he had hoped to make his victims. The packing compound was in his brain, carried there by his fast-hardening blood. He tore a hole in the ground, climbed upward a meter or so, his thoughts upon destruction. To claw and bite was his reality and he needed to feel Kam Shar and Roxey against him, desired to know them intimately. His great will tried to give him what he needed by helping him to move a little farther up the tier. He was grateful that the two shriekers weren't moving at all but were simply standing there waiting for him to arrive.

He found himself staring up at the ceiling. He was rapidly losing sensation, so much so that he didn't feel the pain in his eyes, didn't know they bulged out of his head like dim light bulbs. His stomach was greatly out of proportion, and in fact his entire body was so heavy that he couldn't crawl.

He lay quietly for a while only to discover that he could no longer move. Soon he wouldn't be able to breathe. A felled leviathan, he lay on the gouged-out tier with his gaze fastened upon the unearthly face of the man who had killed him.

DAW PRESENTS MARION ZIMMER BRADLEY

☐ **STORMQUEEN!**
"A novel of the planet Darkover set in the Ages of Chaos
. . . this is richly textured, well-thought-out and involving."
—Publishers Weekly.   (#UJ1381—$1.95)

☐ **HUNTERS OF THE RED MOON**
"May be even more of a treat for devoted MZB fans than
her excellent Darkover series . . . sf adventure in the grand
tradition."—Luna.   (#UE1568—$1.75)

☐ **THE SHATTERED CHAIN**
"Primarily concerned with the role of women in the Darkover
society . . . Bradley's gift is provocative, a top-notch blend
of sword-and-sorcery and the finest speculative fiction."—
Wilson Library Bulletin.   (#UE1566—$2.25)

☐ **THE HERITAGE OF HASTUR**
"A rich and highly colorful tale of politics and magic, cour-
age and pressure . . . Topflight adventure in every way."
—Analog. "May well be Bradley's masterpiece."—Newsday.
"It is a triumph."—Science Fiction Review. (#UJ1307—$1.95)

☐ **DARKOVER LANDFALL**
"Both literate and exciting, with much of that searching
fable quality that made **Lord of the Flies** so provocative."
—New York Times. The novel of Darkover's origin.
                                          (#UE1567—$1.75)

☐ **TWO TO CONQUER**
A novel of the last days of the Age of Chaos and the ulti-
mate conflict.   (#UE1540—$2.25)

☐ **THE KEEPER'S PRICE**
New stories of all the ages of Darkover written by MZB and
members of the Friends of Darkover.   (#UE1517—$2.25)

───────────────────────────────────────

DAW BOOKS are represented by the publishers of Signet
and Mentor Books, THE NEW AMERICAN LIBRARY, INC.

───────────────────────────────────────

THE NEW AMERICAN LIBRARY, INC.,
P.O. Box 999, Bergenfield, New Jersey 07621

Please send me the DAW BOOKS I have checked above. I am enclosing
$_____ (check or money order—no currency or C.O.D.'s).
Please include the list price plus 50¢ per order to cover mailing costs.

Name _____

Address _____

City _____ State _____ Zip Code _____
Please allow at least 4 weeks for delivery